In Favor
of the
Sensitive Man
and Other
Essays

Works by Anaïs Nin

Published by the Swallow Press

D. H. Lawrence: An Unprofessional Study
House of Incest (a prose poem)
Winter of Artifice
Under a Glass Bell (stories)
Ladders to Fire
Children of the Albatross
The Four-Chambered Heart
A Spy in the House of Love
Solar Barque
Seduction of the Minotaur
Collages
Cities of the Interior
A Woman Speaks

Published by Harcourt Brace Jovanovich

The Diary of Anaïs Nin, 1931–1934
The Diary of Anaïs Nin, 1934–1939
The Diary of Anaïs Nin, 1939–1944
The Diary of Anaïs Nin, 1944–1947
The Diary of Anaïs Nin, 1947–1955
The Diary of Anaïs Nin, 1955–1966
A Photographic Supplement to the Diary of Anaïs Nin
In Favor of the Sensitive Man and Other Essays
Delta of Venus: Erotica by Anaïs Nin

Published by Macmillan

The Novel of the Future

Anaïs Nin

In Favor of the Sensitive Man and Other Essays

A Harvest/HBJ Book

Harcourt Brace Jovanovich

New York and London

"My Sister, My Spouse" is from the Norton Library Edition of
My Sister, My Spouse: A Biography of Lou Andreas-Salomé,
by H. F. Peters, and is reprinted with permission of
W. W. Norton & Company, Inc. The author also wishes to thank
the following copyright holders for permission to reprint
these essays: The New York Times Company for "Between Me
and Life," © 1974 by The New York Times Company, and
"Novelist on Stage," © 1966 by The New York Times Company;
The Village Voice, Inc. for "The Suicide Academy,"
copyright © The Village Voice, Inc., 1968, and "The Spirit
of Bali," copyright © The Village Voice, Inc., 1975.

Printed in the United States of America

Library of Congress Cataloging in Publication Data

Nin, Anaïs, date
  In favor of the sensitive man, and other essays.

  (An Original harvest book ; HB 333)
  I. Title.
PS3527.I865I5   814'.5'2   75-38583
ISBN 0-15-644445-3

First Harvest edition 1976
  C D E F G H I J

Contents

Enchanted Places

Women
and Men

Eroticism
in Women

From my personal observation, I would say that woman has not made the separation between love and sensuality which man has made. The two are usually combined in woman; she needs either to love the man she gives herself to or to be loved by him. After lovemaking, she seems to need the assurance that it is love and that the act of sexual possession is part of an exchange which is dictated by love. Men complain that women demand reassurance or expressions of love. The Japanese recognized this need, and in ancient times it was an absolute rule that after a night of lovemaking, the man had to produce a poem and have it delivered to his love before she awakened. What was this but the linking of lovemaking to love?

I believe women still mind a precipitated departure, a lack of acknowledgement of the ritual which has taken place; they still need the words, the telephone call, the letter, the gestures which make the sensual act a particular one, not anonymous and purely sexual.

This may or may not disappear in modern woman, intent on denying all of her past selves, and she may achieve this separation of sex and love which, to my belief, diminishes

From *Playgirl*, April 1974.

pleasure and reduces the heightened quality of lovemaking. For lovemaking is enhanced, heightened, intensified by its emotional content. You might compare the difference to a solo player and the vast reaches of an orchestra.

We are all engaged in the task of peeling off the false selves, the programmed selves, the selves created by our families, our culture, our religions. It is an enormous task because the history of women has been as incompletely told as the history of the blacks. Facts have been obscured. Some cultures such as the Indian, Cambodian, Chinese, and Japanese have made their sensual life very accessible and familiar through their male artists. But many times, when women have wanted to reveal the facets of their sensuality, they have been suppressed. Not in as obvious a way as the burning of D. H. Lawrence's works, or the banning of Henry Miller or James Joyce, but in one long, continuous disparagement by the critics. Many women resorted to using men's names for their work to bypass prejudice. Only a few years ago, Violette Leduc wrote the most explicit, eloquent, moving descriptions of love between women. She was introduced to her public by Simone de Beauvoir. Yet every review I read was a moral judgment upon her openness. There was no moral judgment passed upon the behavior of Henry Miller's characters, merely an objection to language. In the case of Violette Leduc it was upon the character herself.

Violette Leduc in *La Bâtarde* is utterly free:

Isabelle pulled me backwards, she laid me down on the eider-down, she raised me up, she kept me in her arms: she was taking me out of a world where I had never lived so that she could launch me into a world I had not yet reached; the lips opened mine a little, they moistened my teeth. The too fleshy tongue frightened me; but the strange virility didn't force its way in. Absently, calmly, I waited. The lips roved over my lips.

My heart was beating too hard and I wanted to prolong the sweetness of the imprint, the new experience brushing at my lips. Isabelle is kissing me, I said to myself. She was tracing a circle around my mouth, she was encircling the disturbance, she laid a cool kiss in each corner, two staccato notes of music on my lips; then her mouth pressed against mine once more, hibernating there. . . . We were still hugging each other, we both wanted to be swallowed up by the other. . . . As Isabelle lay crushed over my gaping heart I wanted to feel her enter it. She taught me to open into flower. . . . Her tongue, her little flame, softened my muscles, my flesh. . . . A flower opened in every pore of my skin. . . .

We have to shed self-consciousness. Women will have to shed their imitation of Henry Miller. It is all very well to treat sensuality with humor, with caricature, with bawdiness, but that is another way of relegating it to the casual, unimportant areas of experience.

Women have been discouraged from revealing their sensual nature. When I wrote *Spy in the House of Love* in 1954, serious critics called Sabina a nymphomaniac. The story of Sabina is that in ten years of married life, she had known two lovers and one platonic friendship with a homosexual. It was the first study of a woman who tries to separate love from sensuality as man does, to seek sensual freedom. It was termed pornographic at the time. One of the "pornographic" passages:

They fled from the eyes of the world, the singer's prophetic, harsh, ovarian prologues. Down the rusty bars of ladders to the undergrounds of the night propitious to the first man and woman at the beginning of the world, where there were no words by which to possess each other, no music for serenades, no presents to court with, no tournaments to impress and force a yielding, no secondary instruments, no adornments, necklaces, crowns to subdue, but only one ritual, a joyous, joyous, joyous, joyous impaling of woman on man's sensual mast.

<hr>

Eroticism in Women

5

Another passage from *Spy*, labeled pornographic by the critics:

His caresses were so delicate that they were almost like a teasing, an evanescent challenge which she feared to respond to as it might vanish. His fingers teased her, and withdrew when they had aroused her, his mouth teased her and then eluded hers, his face and body came so near, espoused her every limb, and then slid away into the darkness. He would seek every curve and nook he could exert the pressure of his warm slender body against and suddenly lie still, leaving her in suspense. When he took her mouth he moved away from her hands, when she answered the pressure of his thighs, he ceased to exert it. Nowhere would he allow a long enough fusion, but tasting every embrace, every area of her body and then deserting it, as if to ignite only and then elude the final welding. A teasing, warm, trembling, elusive short circuit of the senses as mobile and restless as he had been all day, and here at night, with the street lamp revealing their nudity but not his eyes, she was roused to an almost unbearable expectation of pleasure. He had made of her body a bush of roses of Sharon, exfoliating pollen, each prepared for delight.

So long delayed, so long teased that when possession came it avenged the waiting by a long, prolonged, deep thrusting ecstasy.

Women through their confessions reveal a persistent repression. In the diary of George Sand we come upon this incident: Zola courted her and obtained a night of lovemaking. Because she revealed herself as completely unleashed sensually, he placed money on the night table when he left, implying that a passionate woman was a prostitute.

But if you persist in the study of women's sensuality you find what lies at the end of all studies, that there are no generalizations, that there are as many types of women as there are women themselves. One point is established, that the erotic writings of men do not satisfy women, that it is time we write our own, that there is a difference in erotic needs, fantasies, and attitudes. Explicit barracks or clinical language is not exciting to most women. When Henry Miller's first books came out, I predicted women would like them. I thought they would like the honest assertion of desire which was in danger of disappearing in a puritan culture. But they did not respond to the aggressive and brutal language. The *Kama Sutra*, which is an Indian compendium of erotic lore, stresses the need to approach women with sensitivity and romanticism, not to aim directly at physical possession, but to prepare her with romantic courtship. These customs, habits, mores, change from one culture to another and from one country to another. In the first diary by a woman (written in the year 900), the *Tales of Gengi* by Lady Murasaki, the eroticism is extremely subtle, clothed in poetry, and focussed on areas of the body which a Westerner rarely notices: the bare neck showing between the dark hair and the kimono.

There is common agreement about only one thing, that woman's erogenous zones are spread all over her body, that she is more sensitive to caresses, and that her sensuality is rarely as direct, as immediate as man's. There is an atmosphere of vibrations which need to be awakened and have repercussions on the final arousal.

The feminist Kate Millett is unjust to Lawrence. Whatever he asserted ideologically, she was not subtle enough to see that in his work, which is where the true self is revealed, he was very concerned with the response of woman.

My favorite passage is from *Lady Chatterley's Lover:*

Then as he began to move, in the sudden helpless orgasm, there awoke in her new strange thrills rippling inside her. Rippling, rippling, rippling, like a flapping overlapping of soft flames, soft as feathers, running to points of brilliance, exquisite, exquisite and melting her all molten inside. It was like bells rippling up and up to culmination. She lay unconscious of the wild little cries she uttered at the last. . . . she felt the soft bud of him within her stirring, and strange rhythms flushing up into her with a strange rhythmic growing motion, swelling and swelling till it filled all her cleaving consciousness, and then began again the unspeakable motion that was not really motion, but pure deepening whirlpools of sensation swirling deeper and deeper through all her tissue and consciousness, till she was one perfect concentric fluid of feeling, and she lay there crying in unconscious inarticulate cries. The voice out of the uttermost night, the life!

It was a disillusion, in our modern times, to discover that women courting each other did not necessarily adopt more sensuous, more subtle ways of winning desire, but proceeded with the same aggressive, direct attack as men.

Personally this is what I believe: that brutal language such as Marlon Brando uses in *Last Tango in Paris*, far from affecting woman, repulses her. It disparages, vulgarizes sensuality, it expresses only how the puritan saw it, as low, evil, and dirty. It is a reflection of puritanism. It does not arouse desire. It bestializes sexuality. I find most women object to that as a destruction of eroticism. Among ourselves, we have made the distinction between pornography and eroticism. Pornography treats sexuality grotesquely to bring it back to the animal level. Eroticism arouses sensuality without this need to animalize it. And most of the women I have discussed this with agree they want to develop erotic writing quite distinct from man's. The stance of male writers does not appeal to women. The hunter, the rapist, the one for whom sexuality is a thrust, nothing more.

Linking eroticism to emotion, to love, to a selection of a certain person, personalizing, individualizing, that will be the work of women. There will be more and more women writers who will write out of their own feelings and experiences.

The discovery of woman's erotic capacities and the expression of them will come as soon as women stop listing their griefs against men. If they do not like the hunt, the pursuit, it is up to them to express what they do like and to reveal to men, as they did in oriental tales, the delights of other forms of love games. For the moment their writings are negative. We only hear of what they do not like. They repudiate the role of seduction, of charm, of all the means of bringing about the atmosphere of eroticism they dream about. How can man even become aware of a woman's all-over-the-body sensitivity when it is covered by jeans, which make her body seem like those of his cronies, seemingly with only one aperture of penetration? If it is true that woman's eroticism is spread all over her body, then her way of dressing today is an absolute denial of this factor.

Now, there are women who are restive with the passive role allotted to them. There are women who dream of taking, invading, possessing as man does. It is the liberating force of our awareness today that we would like to start anew and give each woman her own individual pattern, not a generalized one. I wish there were a sensitive computer which could make for each woman a pattern born of her own unconscious desires. It is the exciting adventure we are engaged in. To question all the histories, statistics, confessions, autobiographies, and biographies, and to create our own individual pattern. For this we are obliged to accept what our culture has so long denied, the need of an individual introspective examination. This alone will bring out the women we are, our reflexes, likes, dislikes, and we will go forth without guilt or hesitations, towards the fulfillment of them. There is a type of man who sees lovemaking as we do; there is at least one for each woman. But first of all, we have to know who we are, what are the habits and fantasies of our bodies, the dictates of our imagination. We not only have to recognize what moves, stirs, arouses us, but how to reach it, attain it. At this point I would say woman knows very little about herself. And in the end, she has to make her own erotic pattern and fulfillment through a huge amount of half-information and half-revelations.

Puritanism hangs heavily on American literature. It is what makes the male writers write about sexuality as a low, vulgar, animalistic vice. Some women writers have imitated men, not knowing what other model to follow. All they succeeded in doing was in reversing roles: Women would behave as men have, make love and leave in the morning without a word of tenderness, or any promise of continuity. Woman became the predator, the aggressor. But nothing was ultimately changed by this. We still need to know how women feel, and they will have to express it in writing.

Young women are getting together to explore their sensuality, to dissipate inhibitions. A young instructor of literature, Tristine Rainer, invited several students at UCLA to discuss erotic writing, to examine why they were so inhibited in describing their feelings. The sense of taboo was strong. As soon as they were able to tell each other their fantasies, their wishes, their actual experiences, the writing, too, was liberated. These young women are seeking new patterns because they are aware that their imitation of men is not leading to freedom. The French were able to produce very beautiful erotic writing because there was no puritan taboo, and the best writers would turn to erotic writing without the feeling that sensuality was something to be ashamed of and treated with contempt.

What we will have to reach, the ideal, is the recognition of woman's sensual nature, the acceptance of its needs, the

---

knowledge of the variety of temperaments, and the joyous attitude towards it as a part of nature, as natural as the growth of a flower, the tides, the movements of planets. Sensuality as nature, with possibilities of ecstasy and joy. In Zen terms, with possibility of sartori. We are still under the oppressive puritan rule. The fact that women write about sexuality does not mean liberation. They write about it with the same vulgarization and lower-depths attitude as men. They do not write with pride and joy.

The true liberation of eroticism lies in accepting the fact that there are a million facets to it, a million forms of eroticism, a million objects of it, situations, atmospheres, and variations. We have, first of all, to dispense with guilt concerning its expansion, then remain open to its surprises, varied expressions, and (to add my personal formula for the full enjoyment of it) fuse it with individual love and passion for a particular human being, mingle it with dreams, fantasies, and emotion for it to attain its highest potency. There may have been a time of collective rituals, when sensual release attained its apogee, but we are no longer engaged in collective rituals, and the stronger the passion is for one individual, the more concentrated, intensified, and ecstatic the ritual of one to one can prove to be.

The New
Woman

Why one writes is a question I can answer easily, having so
often asked it of myself. I believe one writes because one
has to create a world in which one can live. I could not live
in any of the worlds offered to me—the world of my parents, the world of war, the world of politics. I had to create
a world of my own, like a climate, a country, an atmosphere
in which I could breathe, reign, and recreate myself when
destroyed by living. That, I believe, is the reason for every
work of art.

The artist is the only one who knows that the world is a
subjective creation, that there is a choice to be made, a
selection of elements. It is a materialization, an incarnation
of his inner world. Then he hopes to attract others into it.
He hopes to impose his particular vision and share it with
others. And when the second stage is not reached, the brave
artist continues nevertheless. The few moments of communion with the world are worth the pain, for it is a world for
others, an inheritance for others, a gift to others in the end.

We also write to heighten our own awareness of life. We
write to lure and enchant and console others. We write to

A lecture given at the Celebration of Women in the Arts, in San
Francisco, April 1974; first published in *Ramparts*, June 1974.

serenade our lovers. We write to taste life twice, in the moment and in retrospection. We write, like Proust, to render all of it eternal, and to persuade ourselves that it is eternal. We write to be able to transcend our life, to reach beyond it. We write to teach ourselves to speak with others, to record the journey into the labyrinth. We write to expand our world when we feel strangled, or constricted, or lonely. We write as the birds sing, as the primitives dance their rituals. If you do not breathe through writing, if you do not cry out in writing, or sing in writing, then don't write, because our culture has no use for it. When I don't write, I feel my world shrinking. I feel I am in a prison. I feel I lose my fire and my color. It should be a necessity, as the sea needs to heave, and I call it breathing.

For too many centuries women have been busy being muses to the artists. And I know you have followed me in the diary when I wanted to be a muse, and I wanted to be the wife of the artist, but I was really trying to avoid the final issue—that I had to do the job myself. In letters I've received from women, I've found what Rank had described as a guilt for creating. It's a very strange illness, and it doesn't strike men—because the culture has demanded of man that he give his maximum talents. He is encouraged by the culture, to become the great doctor, the great philosopher, the great professor, the great writer. Everything is really planned to push him in that direction. Now, this was not asked of women. And in my family, just as in your family probably, I was expected simply to marry, to be a wife, and to raise children. But not all women are gifted for that, and sometimes, as D. H. Lawrence properly said, "We don't need more children in the world, we need hope."

So this is what I set out to do, to adopt all of you. Because Baudelaire told me a long time ago that in each one of us there is a man, a woman, and a child—and the child is always in trouble. The psychologists are always confirming what the poets have said so long ago. You know, even poor, maligned Freud said once, "Everywhere I go, I find a poet has been there before me." So the poet said we have three personalities, and one was the child fantasy which remained in the adult and which, in a way, makes the artist.

When I talk so much of the artist, I don't mean only the one who gives us music, who gives us color, who gives us architecture, who gives us philosophy, who gives us so much and enriches our life. I mean the creative spirit in all its manifestations. For me even as a child, when my father and mother were quarreling—my father was a pianist and my mother was a singer—when music time came, everything became peaceful and beautiful. And as children we shared the feeling that music was a magical thing which restored harmony in the family and made life bearable for us.

Now, there was a woman in France—and I give her story because it shows how we can turn and metamorphose and use everything to become creative. This was the mother of Utrillo. Because she was very poor, the mother of Utrillo was condemned to be a laundress and a houseworker. But she lived in Montmartre at the time of almost the greatest group of painters that was ever put together, and she became a model for them. As she watched the painters paint, she learned to paint. And she became, herself, a noted painter, Suzanne Valadon. It was the same thing that happened to me when I was modelling at the age of sixteen, because I didn't have any profession and I didn't know how else to earn a living. I learned from the painters the sense of color, which was to train me in observation my whole life.

I learned many things from the artist which I would call creating out of nothing. Varda, for example, taught me that collage is made out of little bits of cloth. He even had me cut a piece of the lining of my coat because he took a liking to the color of it and wanted to incorporate it into a collage. He was making very beautiful celestial gardens and fantasies of every possible dream with just little bits of cloth and glue. Varda is also the one who taught me that if you leave a chair long enough on the beach, it becomes bleached into the most beautiful color imaginable which you could never find with paint.

I learned from Tinguely that he went to junkyards, and he picked out all kinds of bits and pieces of machines and built some machines which turned out to be caricatures of technology. He even built a machine which committed suicide, which I described in a book called *Collages*. I am trying to say that the artist is a magician—that he taught me that no matter where you are put, you can always somehow come out of that place.

Now, I was placed somewhere you might imagine would be terribly interesting, a suburb of Paris. But a suburb of Paris can be just as lonely as a suburb of New York or Los Angeles or San Francisco. I was in my twenties and I didn't know anyone at the time, so I turned to my love of writers. I wrote a book, and suddenly I found myself in a Bohemian, artistic, literary writer's world. And that was my bridge. But sometimes, when people say to me, that's fine, but you were gifted for writing, my answer is that there is not always that kind of visible skill.

I know a woman who started with nothing, whom I consider a great heroine. She had not been able to go to high school because her family was very poor and had so many children. The family lived on a farm in Saratoga, but she decided to go to New York City. She began working at Brentano's and after a little while told them that she wanted to have a bookshop of her own. They laughed at her and said that she was absolutely mad and would never survive the summer. She had $150 saved and she rented a little place that went downstairs in the theater section of New York, and everybody came in the evening after the theater. And today her bookshop is not only the most famous bookshop in New York, the Gotham Book Mart, but it is a place where everybody wants to have bookshop parties. She has visitors from all over the world—Edith Sitwell came to see her when she came to New York, Jean Cocteau, and many more. And no other bookshop in New York has that fascination, which comes from her, her humanity and friendliness, and the fact that people can stand there and read a book and she won't even notice them. Frances Steloff is her name, and I mention her whenever anyone claims that it takes a particular skill to get out of a restricted, limited, or impoverished life. Frances is now eighty-six, a beautiful old lady with white hair and perfect skin who has defied age.

It was the principle of creative will that I admired and learned from musicians like Eric Satie, who defied starvation and used his compositions to protect his piano from the dampness of his little room in a suburb of Paris. Even Einstein, who disbelieved Newton's unified field theory, died believing what is being proved now. I give that as an instance of faith, and faith is what I want to talk about. What kept me writing, when for twenty years I was received by complete silence, is that faith in the necessity to be the artist—and no matter what happens even if there is no one listening.

I don't need to speak of Zelda Fitzgerald. I think all of you have thought about Zelda, how she might never have lost her mind if Fitzgerald had not forbidden her to publish her diary. It is well known that Fitzgerald said no, that it could not be published, because he would need it for his own work. This, to me, was the beginning of Zelda's disturbance. She was unable to fulfill herself as a writer and was overpowered by the reputation of Fitzgerald. But if you read her own book, you will find that in a sense she created a much more original novel than he ever did, one more modern in its effort to use language in an original way.

History, much like the spotlight, has hit whatever it wanted to hit, and very often it missed the woman. We all know about Dylan Thomas. Very few of us know about Caitlin Thomas, who after her husband's death wrote a book which is a poem in itself and sometimes surpasses his own—in strength, in primitive beauty, in a real wakening of feeling. But she was so overwhelmed by the talent of Dylan Thomas that she never thought anything of her writing at all until he died.

So we're here to celebrate the sources of faith and confidence. I want to give you the secrets of the constant alchemy that we must practice to turn brass into gold, hate into love, destruction into creation—to change the crass daily news into inspiration, and despair into joy. None need misinterpret this as indifference to the state of the world or to the actions by which we can stem the destructiveness of the corrupt system. There is an acknowledgement that, as human beings, we need nourishment to sustain the life of the spirit, so that we can act in the world, but I don't mean turn away. I mean we must gain our strength and our values from self-growth and self-discovery. Against all odds, against all handicaps, against the chamber of horrors we call history, man has continued to dream and to depict its opposite. That is what we have to do. We do not escape into philosophy, psychology, and art—we go there to restore our shattered selves into whole ones.

The woman of the future, who is really being born today, will be a woman completely free of guilt for creating and for her self-development. She will be a woman in harmony with her own strength, not necessarily called masculine, or eccentric, or something unnatural. I imagine she will be very tranquil about her strength and her serenity, a woman who will know how to talk to children and to the men who sometimes fear her. Man has been uneasy about this self-evolution of woman, but he need not be—because, instead of having a dependent, he will have a partner. He will have someone who will not make him feel that every day he has to go into battle against the world to support a wife and child, or a childlike wife. The woman of the future will never try to live vicariously through the man, and urge and push him to despair, to fulfill something that she should really be doing herself. So that is my first image—she is not aggressive, she is serene, she is sure, she is confident, she is able to develop her skills, she is able to ask for space for herself.

I want this quality of the sense of the person, the sense of direct contact with human beings to be preserved by woman, not as something bad, but as something that could make a totally different world where intellectual capacity would be fused with intuition and with a sense of the personal.

Now, when I wrote the diary and when I wrote fiction, I was trying to say that we need both intimacy and a deep knowledge of a few human beings. We also need mythology and fiction which is a little further away, and art is always a little further away from the entirely personal world of the woman. But I want to tell you the story of Colette. When her name was suggested for the Académie française, which is considered the highest honor given to writers, there was much discussion because she hadn't written about war, she hadn't written about any large event, she had only written about love. They admired her as a writer, as a stylist—she was one of our best stylists—but somehow the personal world of Colette was not supposed to have been very important. And I think it is extremely important, because we have lost that intimacy and that person-to-person sense, which she developed because she had been more constricted and less active in the world. So the family was very important, the neighbor was very important, and the friend was very important.

It would be nice if men could share that too, of course. And they will, on the day they recognize the femininity in themselves, which is what Jung has been trying to tell us. I was asked once how I felt about men who cried, and I said that I loved men who cried, because it showed they had feeling. The day that woman admits what we call her masculine qualities, and man admits his so-called feminine qualities, will mean that we admit we are androgynous, that we have many personalities, many sides to fulfill. A woman can be courageous, can be adventurous, she can be all these things. And this new woman who is coming up is very inspiring, very wonderful. And I love her.

Anaïs Nin Talks About Being a Woman: An Interview

QUESTIONER: Are you surprised by your rediscovery by the young and your power as a force with them?

ANAÏS NIN: The young, after all, were the first to come to me after my return from Europe at the beginning of World War II. The young find in me a similarity in attitude—living with the senses, intuition, magic, using the psychic, an awareness of a different set of values. They find in me a primary interest in life and intimacy, in knowing each other. When I lecture in colleges, I talk about *furrawn*, a Welsh word that means the kind of talk that leads to intimacy. We talk about their lives and personal things, and then they open up to me. At first, I wondered why they wanted me to lecture and now I realize they simply wanted to see if I were real.

Q: Kate Millett in her controversial book *Sexual Politics* attacks your friend Henry Miller for the way he, a male writer, has influenced our thinking about sex. Because of your intimacy with and support of Miller, do you feel you compromised yourself as a woman?

AN: Not at all. He was my opposite. As I wrote in my

From *Vogue*, 15 October 1971.

diary, I didn't like his attitude towards sex. But even Freud behaved entirely differently with Lou Andreas-Salomé. You see, it's a matter of the woman. Miller treated me differently. I took his antipuritanism as comic. By asserting his appetites, he changed both men and women. I think I saw Miller very clearly, but I don't feel now I have to attack or defend him. Miller did a lot to remove the puritanical superstitions of other men. At that moment, women were inaccessible. He brought them nearer. He made them real.

Q: You observed once you had not "imitated man." What role do men have in your work?

AN: No, I didn't imitate men. Men, for me, were doctor, psychiatrist, astronomer, astrologer. It was their knowledge I needed. I followed men in everything creative, but I sought always to strengthen and reveal the pattern of women. Women were my patterns for living, men for thinking. When I was thirteen and fourteen, Joan of Arc was my heroine. After all, she went to war for a man and not for herself. There are so few women who have found real freedom for themselves. I think of Ninon de Lenclos in the seventeenth century and Lou Andreas-Salomé in the nineteenth. The symbolic people and their freedom are important to the new consciousness. Women must stop reacting against what *is*. They should be making the new woman very clear to us.

Q: What for you is the "new woman"?

AN: In my works, I had portrayed free women, free love; but I had done it quietly and these "new women" were not perceived. There is no one pattern for the new woman. She will have to find her own way. This is the work to be done, but it will have to be done individually. Women want a pattern, but there is no pattern for all women.

Anaïs Nin Talks About Being a Woman

Q: Much has been made by Women's Liberation of Freud's biases against women. Did these biases affect you, in your own analysis?

AN: I really can't answer that question. I haven't read Freud in a long time, but I do remember Dr. Otto Rank, who analyzed me in Paris, saying that we didn't really understand the psychology of women, that women had not yet articulated their experience. Men invented soul, philosophy, religion. Women have perceptions that are difficult to describe, at least in intellectual terms. These perceptions come instantly from intuition, and the woman trusts them. What bothers Women's Lib about Freud doesn't bother me. Psychology helped me. I very much felt the inner necessity to grow. The ideologies—as Rank said— may have been made by men, but I used only what was useful to me.

Q: Why has active interest in the erotic been so long taboo for women?

AN: Men must have invented the taboo. I think of Fellini. He dramatized his unconscious life in 8 1/2; but, when he filmed his wife's unconscious life in *Juliet of the Spirits*, he didn't allow her any adventures. She was a passive spectator. For him, woman is only pure by faithfulness and abstention. D. H. Lawrence was the first to acknowledge that woman has a sexuality, a life of her own, and that lovemaking can originate with the woman. Eroticism is one of the basic means of self-knowledge, as indispensable as poetry. But if a woman writes openly about her need—for example, Violette Leduc or Caitlin Thomas, the widow of Dylan Thomas—she is damned.

I have always admitted the sexual appetite and given it a great place in my work. One of my books was called *This Hunger*. Henry Miller did a lot to break the canonization of women. Some women, like men, would rather be treated as sexual objects than be canonized. Women don't like being romanticized or idealized any more than they like being insulted or humiliated.

Q: What are the defining limits of masculinity and femininity?

AN: I have tried to lessen the distinctions. I wanted to show all the relationships and establish the fluid connections beyond sex. I found in literature more descriptions of obstacles than relationships. I was seeking to establish the flow and let all the rest fall into place. I wanted to eliminate boundaries, taboos, limitations. In the old novels, there were the differences of class, race, religion. I wanted to leap over all that and reach the instinctive and intuitive connections.

Q: What for you is the contrast between the feeling life of men and women?

AN: They meet. There is a resemblance between men and women, not a contrast. When a man begins to recognize his feeling, the two unite. When men *accept* the sensitive side of themselves, they come alive. Analysis we've always thought of as masculine—that was the area in which I was able to talk to men. But all those differences are disappearing. We speak of the masculine and the feminine, but they are the wrong labels. It is really more a matter of poetry versus intellectualization.

Q: When you were twenty-nine, you wrote that there were two women in you: "one woman desperate and bewildered, who felt she was drowning, and another who would leap into a scene, as upon a stage, conceal her true emotions because they were weaknesses, helplessness, and despair, and present to the world only a smile, an eagerness, curiosity, enthusiasm, interest." How did you master yourself?

AN: One continually leaps over the negative. I haven't yet

reached a point where I'm courageous every day. And the struggle keeps my diary alive. Now I have a sense of harmony, of integration. I feel free. The two women are there in me, but they don't tear at each other. They live in peace.

Q: How did you achieve this integration?

AN: I started out terribly engrossed in dreams, the spiritual, the reverie. My father's leaving us when I was nine shattered me. I had lived in books and imagination, so my journey into my self was different. I had to find the earth. My father's leaving gave me the feeling of a broken bridge with the world that I wanted to rebuild. For me, everything came from literature: the lies, the stories, the dreams. Then, Henry Miller and his wife came into my life. In my thirties, I was concerned with experience, and I wrote my first book on D. H. Lawrence. When I had balanced the two worlds—earth and imagination—then came the period of the greatest creativity. I began to produce almost a book a year. At this stage in my life, the diary and fiction, the poetry and earth, are in harmony. I can work and travel and have relationships without conflict.

Q: What is the story of your famous diary?

AN: I began the diary at the age of eleven on the ship coming to America, separated from my father, to describe to him this strange land and entice him to come. It would enable him to follow our lives. The diary was begun to bring someone back. My mother didn't let me mail it; and it became private, a house of the spirit, a laboratory. It became a refuge, a sanctuary. Now, there are perhaps two hundred volumes. I write perhaps twelve a year. I store them in filing cabinets in a bank vault in Brooklyn that costs fifty dollars every three months.

Q: In an important sense, you are a revolutionary. What have you learned about yourself and other women through your solitary courage?

AN: The importance of faith, the great importance of orientation and the inner life to withstand outer pressures. Also, the understanding that increased awareness *will* prevail and cause external changes. The importance of inner conviction. I had the love of my work and nothing could stop it.

Q: Many critics have been alarmed by the highly charged atmosphere of your writing. Why are mystery, allure, and intrigue so often the weapons of your heroines?

AN: I think it's because I believe in communicating by way of the emotions, by imagery, indirectness, the myth. I think all my women have tried to live by the impulses of the subconscious. In all my novels, I have only one heroine in direct action, and even she discovers the necessity of the inner journey. I never believed in action, only in achieving life on a poetic level.

Q: Love has always been the crucial issue for you in both your novels and diaries, but you seldom speak of it in an uncomplicated way. Why do you find love such an intricate mesh of relationships?

AN: Love is complex. Because of the obstacles, personas, masks, a relationship is an arduous creation. Human beings construct labyrinths. If we live out all our selves, that becomes a very intricate pattern. But we have to keep a balance perpetually, the constant oscillations I try to describe.

Q: The intuition is deeply a part of your novelistic method. Can you describe your fascination with divination in all its forms?

AN: As a child, I was intensely aware of what people felt; I tried to confirm my intuition by studying psychology. My tendency to romanticize made me want to verify what I felt. Now I trust my intuition and its strength. When I was in Japan, I had a sense of contact with people who speak a language I do not speak. Intuition was my divination, but in my novels and my life I expanded my intuition. In Louveciennes in the thirties, I had an attic studio with steeply inclined ceilings. Between the windows, we painted the horoscopes of all our friends and followed them day by day. Each horoscope had hands like a clock and we arranged them in configurations of each day so we could study them and say "Artaud's horoscope today is . . ." I'm no longer interested in the predictive side of astrology but rather in what it has to say about character. At the same time as we began following the charts, I imitated the form of the astrological charts and arranged my friends and their cities in constellations. I very much liked the idea of relationships being visualized as horoscopes and charts.

Notes on
Feminism

The nature of my contribution to the Women's Liberation Movement is not political but psychological. I get thousands of letters from women who have been liberated by the reading of my diaries, which are a long study of the psychological obstacles that have prevented woman from her fullest evolution and flowering. I studied the negative influence of religion, of racial and cultural patterns, which action alone and no political slogans can dissolve. I describe in the diaries the many restrictions confining woman. The diary itself was an escape from judgment, a place in which to analyze the truth of woman's situation. I believe that is where the sense of freedom has to begin. I say begin, not remain. A reformation of woman's emotional attitudes and beliefs will enable her to act more effectively. I am not speaking of the practical, economic, sociological problems, as I believe many of them are solvable with clear thinking and intelligence. I am merely placing the emphasis on a confrontation of ourselves because it is a source of strength. Do not confuse my shifting of responsibility with blame. I am not blaming woman. I say that if we take the responsibility for our situation, we can feel less helpless

From *The Massachusetts Review,* Winter–Spring 1972.

than when we put the blame on society or man. We waste precious energy in negative rebellions. Awareness can give us a sense of captainship over our fate, and to take destiny into our own hands is more inspiring than to expect others to direct our destiny for us. No matter what ideas, psychology, history, or art I learned from man, I learned to convert it into the affirmation of my own identity and my own beliefs, to serve my own growth. At the same time, I loved woman and was fully aware of her problems, and I watched her struggles for development. I believe the lasting revolution comes from deep changes in ourselves which influence our collective life.

Many of the chores women accepted were ritualistic; they were means of expressing love and care and protection. We have to find other ways of expressing these devotions. We cannot solve the problem of freeing ourselves of all chores without first understanding why we accomplished them and felt guilty when we did not. We have to persuade those we love that there are other ways of enriching their lives. Part of these occupations were compensatory. The home was our only kingdom, and it returned many pleasures. We were repaid with love and beauty and a sense of accomplishment. If we want our energy and strength to go into other channels, we have to work at a transitional solution which may deprive us of a personal world altogether. But I also think we have to cope with our deep-seated, deeply instilled sense of responsibility. That means finding a more creative way of love and collaboration, of educating our children, or caring for a house, and we have to convince those we love that there are other ways of accomplishing these things. The restrictions of women's lives, confined to the personal, also created in us qualities men lost to a degree in a competitive world. I think woman retains a more human relationship to human beings and is not corrupted by the impersonality of powerful interests. I have watched woman in law, in politics, and in education. Because of her gift for personal relationships she deals more effectively with injustice, war, prejudice. I have a dream about woman pouring into all professions a new quality. I want a different world, not the same world born of man's need of power which is the origin of war and injustice. We have to create a new woman.

What of ghettos and poverty? A new kind of human being would not allow them to be born in the first place. It is the quality of human beings I want to see improved, because we already know that drugs, crime, war, and injustice are not curable by a change of system. It is humanism which is lacking in our leaders. I do not want to see women follow in the same pattern. To assert individual qualities and thought was tabooed by puritanism and is now being equally tabooed by militant fanatics. But practical problems are often solved by psychological liberation. The imagination, the skills, the intelligence, are freed to discover solutions. I see so many women in the movement thinking in obsessional circles about problems which are solvable when one is emotionally free to think and act clearly. Undirected, blind anger and hostility are not effective weapons. They have to be converted into lucid action. Each woman has to consider her own problems before she can act effectively within her radius; otherwise she is merely adding the burden of her problems to the collective overburdened majority. Her individual solution, courage, become in turn like cellular growth, organic growth. It is added to the general synthesis. Slogans do not give strength because generalizations are untrue. Many intelligent women, many potentially collaborative men, are alienated by generalizations. To recruit all women for a work for which some are unfit is not effective. The group does not always give strength, because it moves only according to the lowest denominator of understanding. The group weakens the individual will and annihilates the individual contribution. To object to individual growth of awareness in women is to work against the benefit of the collective whose quality is raised by individual research and learning. Each woman has to know herself, her problems, her obstacles. I ask woman to realize she can be master of her own destiny. This is an inspiring thought. To blame others means one feels helpless. What I liked best about psychology is the concept that destiny is interior, in our own hands. While we wait for others to free us, we will not develop the strength to do it ourselves. When a woman has not solved her personal, intimate defeats, her private hostilities, her failures, she brings the dregs of this to the group and only increases its negative reactions. This is placing liberation on too narrow a basis. Liberation means the power to transcend obstacles. The obstacles are educational, religious, racial, and cultural patterns. These have to be confronted, and there is no political solution which serves them all. The real tyrants are guilt, taboos, educational inheritance—these are our enemies. And we can grapple with them. The real enemy is what we were taught, not always by man, but often by our mothers and grandmothers.

The trouble with anger is that it makes us overstate our case and prevents us from reaching awareness. We often damage our case by anger. It is like resorting to war.

Poverty and injustice and prejudice are not solved by any man-made system. I want them to be solved by a higher quality of human being who, by his own law of valuation upon human life, will not permit such inequalities. In that sense whatever we do for the development of this higher quality will eventually permeate all society. The belief that all of us, untrained, unprepared and unskilled, can be conscripted for mass action is what has prevented woman from developing, because it is the same old-fashioned assertion that the only good we can do is outside of ourselves, salvaging others. When we do this we ignore the fact that the evil comes from individual flaws, undeveloped human beings. We need models. We need heroes and leaders. Out of the many lawyers who came from Harvard, we were given only one Nader. But one Nader has incalculable influence. If we continue in the name of politics to denigrate those who have developed their skills to the maximum pitch as elite, privileged, or exceptional people, we will never be able to help others achieve their potential. We need blueprints for the creation of human beings as well as for architecture.

The attack against individual development belongs to the dark ages of socialism. If I am able to inspire or help women today, it is because I persisted in my development. I was often derailed by other duties, but I never gave up this relentless disciplined creation of my awareness because I realized that at the bottom of every failed system to improve the lot of man lies an imperfect, corruptible human being.

It is inspiring to read of the women who defied the codes and taboos of their period: Ninon de Lenclos in the seventeenth century, Lou Andreas-Salomé in the time of Freud, Nietzsche, and Rilke, and in our time Han Suyin. Or the four heroines of Lesley Blanch's *Wilder Shores of Love*.

I see a great deal of negativity in the Women's Liberation Movement. It is less important to attack male writers than to discover and read women writers, to attack male-dominated films than to make films by women. If the passivity of woman is going to erupt like a volcano or an earthquake, it will not accomplish anything but disaster. This passivity can be converted to creative will. If it expresses itself in war, then it is an imitation of man's methods. It would be good to study the writings of women who were more concerned with personal relationships than with the power struggles of history. I have a dream of a more human lawyer, a more human educator, a more human politician. To become man, or like man, is no solution. There is far too much imitation of man in the women's movement. That is merely a displacement of power. Woman's definition of power should be different. It should be based on relationships to others. The women who truly identify with their oppressors, as the cliché phrase goes, are the women who are acting like men, masculinizing themselves, not those who seek to convert or transform man. There is no liberation of one group at the expense of another. Liberation can only come totally and in unison.

Group thinking does not give strength. It weakens the will. Majority thinking is oppressive because it inhibits individual growth and seeks a formula for all. Individual growth makes communal living of higher quality. A developed woman will know how to take care of all her social duties and how to act effectively.

My Sister, My Spouse

It is thanks to H. F. Peters that I was introduced to Lou Andreas-Salomé, and this preface to the republication of his book is an act of gratitude. He presented a full portrait of her even though not all information about her was available. He was handicapped by her own destruction of many of her letters. But through his sensitivity, understanding, and empathy we acquire an intimate knowledge of a woman whose importance to the history of the development of woman is immeasurable. Peters has done a loving portrait which communicates her talent and her courage.

The lack of complete knowledge of Lou's life forces our imagination to interpret her in the light of woman's struggle for independence. We can accept the mysteries, ambivalences, and contradictions because they are analogous to the state of our knowledge of woman today. There is much to be filled in about the inner motives and reactions, the subconscious drives of women. History and biography have to be rewritten. We do not possess yet a feminine point of view in evaluating woman because of so many years of taboos on revelations. Women were usually punished by

Preface to the Norton Library Edition of *My Sister, My Spouse: A Biography of Lou Andreas-Salomé,* by H. F. Peters.

society and by the critics for such revelations as they did attempt. The double standard in biographies of women was absolute. Peters makes no such judgments. He gives us all the facts we need to interpret her in the light of new evaluations.

Lou Andreas-Salomé symbolizes the struggle to transcend conventions and traditions in ideas and in living. How can an intelligent, creative, original woman relate to men of genius without being submerged by them? The conflict of the woman's wish to merge with the loved one but to maintain a separate identity is the struggle of modern woman. Lou lived out all the phases and evolutions of love, from giving to withholding, from expansion to contraction. She married and led a nonmarried life, she loved both older and younger men. She was attracted to talent but did not want to serve merely as a disciple or a muse. Nietzsche admitted writing *Zarathustra* under her inspiration; he said that she understood his work as no one else did.

For many years she suffered the fate of brilliant women associated with brilliant men: She was known only as the friend of Nietzsche, Rilke, Freud, even though the publication of her correspondence with Freud showed with what equality he treated her and how he sought her opinion with respect. She made the first feminist study of Ibsen's women and a study of Nietzsche's work. But her books are not in print.

If she inspired Rilke, she also rebelled against his dependency and his depressions. Her love of life was weighed down, and finally after six years, she broke with him because as she said, "I cannot be faithful to others, only to myself." She had her own work to do, and her faithfulness was to her expansive nature, her passion for life, and her work. She awakened others' talents, but maintained a space for her own. She behaved as did all the strong personalities of her time whose romantic attachments we all admired *when they were men.* She had a talent for friendship and love, but she was not consumed by the passions of the romantics which made them prefer death to the loss of love. Yet she inspired romantic passions. She was, in attitude, thought, and work, way ahead of her time. All this Peters conveys, suggests, confirms.

It was natural that Lou should fascinate me, haunt me. But I wondered what Lou would mean to a young woman, a creative and modern young woman. That is when I decided to discuss Lou with Barbara Kraft, who writes in a study of Lou:

During the span of Salomé's life (1861–1937) she witnessed the close of the romantic tradition and became a part of the evolution of modern thought which came to fruition in the twentieth century. Salomé was the first "modern woman." The nature of her talks with Nietzsche and Rilke anticipated the philosophical position of existentialism. And through her work with Freud she figured prominently in the early development and practice of psychoanalytical theory. I began to see her as a heroine—as a person worthy of hero worship in its most positive aspects. Women today suffer tremendously from a lack of identification with a heroic feminine figure.

Barbara felt that the feminine heroic figures hardly exist because their biographies are usually written by men. As women we sought women who would give us strength, inspire, and encourage us. This is what Peters's portrait of Lou does.

We discussed why she moved from one relationship to another. We could see that as a very young woman she feared the domination of Nietzsche, who was seeking a disciple, one who would perpetuate *his* work. After reading her letters to Rilke, we could understand why after six years she felt she had fulfilled her relationship to Rilke and had to move on. She showed remarkable persistence in maintaining her identity. Gently and wisely she expressed feminine insights in her discussions with Freud and he came to respect her judgment. She preserved her autonomy while surrounded by powerful, even overpowering men. Because she was a beautiful woman their interest often shifted from admiration to passion; when she did not respond she was termed frigid. Her freedom consisted in acting out her deep unconscious needs. She saw independence as the only way to achieve movement. And for her, movement was constant growth and evolution.

She took her pattern of life from men but she was not a masculine woman. She demanded the freedom to change, to evolve, to grow. She asserted her integrity against sentimentality and hypocritical definitions of loyalties and duties. She is unique in the history of her time. She was not a feminist at all, but struggling against the feminine side of herself in order to maintain her integrity as an individual.

H. F. Peters, who fully understood Lou, quotes her own summation: "Human life—indeed all life—is poetry. We live it unconsciously, day by day, piece by piece, but in its inviolable wholeness it lives us."

Between Me
and Life

In this biography of a highly gifted but little known woman artist, Meryle Secrest combines lucid psychological insight with empathy in a deep exploration of character and relationships. She brings into vivid life a lost segment of art history. She has the skill and power to recreate history in shimmering colors. It is unusual when a study of character probes so deeply within a human being and still paints the atmosphere around it, the life style of the times.

The book is fascinating for many reasons. American-born Romaine Goddard Brooks, who died in 1970 at the age of ninety-six, endured a nightmare childhood which would have stunted and distorted anyone else. The artist developed in spite of it. Even if, in her own words, this childhood stood "between me and life"—like an invisible fog, cooling the temperature of her loves or preventing the fullest expansion of her genius, even interfering with the life impulse—nevertheless, compared to the stunted lives of many modern artists today, she was involved in a rich, color-

A review of *Between Me and Life: A Biography of Romaine Brooks*, by Meryle Secrest, in *The New York Times Book Review*, 24 November 1974.

ful pattern of friendships and loves with many remarkable figures of her time.

Secrest never mentions these artists and writers merely as famous names; each one is fully described and studied. By keeping them under a strong spotlight at the time of their involvement with Romaine Brooks, she keeps a beautiful balance between introducing famous persons and exploring them fully.

The turn of the century in Paris was an era which permitted originality, which tolerated individual patterns of life, eccentricities, all the forms and expressions of love. It was a time when emphasis was on talent.

The history of Natalie Barney, the American heiress, in itself is fruitful, and has as many repercussions as the central theme of lesbian love which united her to Romaine Brooks. They were both talented, independent women who formed their own patterns of life and behavior. The fullness and many dimensions of their relationship created an intense suspense. What enhances our interest in the story of Romaine Brooks is the close, intimate view we get of her remarkable friends—the illusion of living at that time and taking part in achievements and the despair they experience.

"Taken together, the 13 canvases which Romaine Brooks showed at the prestigious Galéries Durand-Ruel six years after her stay in St. Ives, are statements of mature talent and triumphant vindication of her determination to become an artist ('I was born an artist. Née an artist, not née Goddard'), achieved at the cost of a total break with her family, then years of poverty and concentrated effort."

Robert de Montesquieu, the eccentric poet, art critic, and leader of society who had inspired Proust's Baron de Charlus, admired and befriended her and called her a "Thief of Souls" because he felt that in her portraits she captured and revealed the secret, sorrowful self concealed behind the persona. Apollinaire found too much sadness and austerity in her work. Secrest suggests Romaine Brooks may have projected her own tragic imprint upon others, or it may be that her tragic life revealed to her more readily the carefully hidden scars in others.

Jean Cocteau, Paul Morand, Ida Rubinstein, and D'Annunzio posed for her. She was surrounded all her life by significant figures, Somerset Maugham, Axel Munthe, Gertrude Stein, Ezra Pound, André Gide, Colette, Compton Mackenzie. She attempted one marriage with a homosexual on the assumption they could be companions but live out their own preferences. It lasted barely a year.

The quest for love and for fulfillment as an artist are the book's major themes. As an artist she received admiration and recognition from the most discriminating minds in Europe. In the quest for love, what Romaine Brooks wanted, says Secrest, was what she never had, a mother's all-accepting love. Secrest quotes Dr. Charlotte Wolff: "Emotional incest with the mother is indeed the very essence of lesbianism." To my mind that is a limited concept, and any quest for love might be said to be a substitute for the one not given at the beginning of one's life. Secrest reminds us that Dante had a special nook in his inferno for the parents who did not love their children. In the case of Romaine Brooks, the injury was compounded by the obsessional love of the mother for the son, adding to Brooks's conviction that she should deny her femininity.

The deep love affair with Natalie Barney, " 'the wild girl from Cincinnati,' known all over Paris for her wealth, social connections, poetry, aphoristic writings and scandalously unorthodox life," is a fascinating study, complex and fully given. The long relationship with D'Annunzio is equally rich in texture, moods.

Between Me and Life

39

Romaine Brooks's paintings were exhibited for the first time in America in 1971, the year after she died in obscurity in Nice. Secrest writes: "In describing the life of an artist one can consider the work as its own phenomenon, separate from the life, or find its origin in the particular psychic set of the artist. The work of Romaine Brooks cannot be separated from her life."

She is one of the extraordinary women recently rescued from oblivion. This might be attributed to women's increasing awareness of the need to rewrite the history of woman, or to the more mysterious cause which often obscures the works of an artist until our taste, our discernment, our comprehension has caught up with it, explaining the cycles of eclipses and the cycles when an artist long dead becomes a vital part of our modern consciousness. Today we understand much better the excruciating relationship of Romaine Brooks to her insane mother. We understand the multiple and diverse expressions of love, the obstacles and complexities attending the development of a woman artist.

Lord Alfred Douglas sent Romaine Brooks his book of poems inscribed: "We have often told each other imperishable things."

This might be said of this biography, in which the history of painting, of mores, of places, of people is harmoniously interwoven, and following the Ariadne thread of one life deeply enough will allow us to discover many lives and imperishable depths of experience.

Women and Children of Japan

The women of Japan are at once the most present and the most invisible and elusive inhabitants of any country I have seen. They are everywhere—in restaurants, streets, shops, museums, subways, trains, fields, hotels, and inns—and yet achieve a self-effacement which is striking to foreign women. In the hotels and inns they are solicitous, thoughtful, helpful to a degree never dreamed of except by men, but this care and tenderness are lavished equally on women visitors. It is as if one's dream of an ever-attentive, ever-protective mother were fulfilled on a collective scale, only the mother is forever young and daintily dressed. They are laborious and yet quiet, efficient, ever-present and yet not intrusive or cumbersome.

I was invited to Japan by my publisher, Tomohisa Kawade, and being a writer, was allowed at the geisha restaurant where the patrons are usually only men. A geisha kneeled or stood behind each guest, and no sooner was my saki cup empty than my geisha leaned forward in the swiftest and lightest gesture and filled it again. She also noticed I did not know how to handle my fish with chopsticks, so she operated on it with amazing skill. She softened the fish
From the diary of Anaïs Nin.

first with pressure from the chopsticks, and then suddenly pulled the entire bone clean and free. All this in an exquisite dress with floating sleeves, which would paralyze a Western woman. Another geisha brought me her scarf to sign: "I have read Hemingway," she said, "he signed my scarf when I was fifteen years old."

They stoop before you not a moment longer than necessary; not one of them seemed to be saying: Look at me; I am here. How they carried trays and served food and listened seemed like a miraculous triumph over clumsiness, perspiration, heaviness. They had conquered gravitation.

Dressed as they were, in fresh and embroidered kimonos, with their hair in the classical coiffure, lacquered and neat, with their white tabi and new sandals, it hurt me to see them follow us out into the street, in the rain, and bow low in the rain until we were away.

Outside of Tokyo, I saw them in their geisha quarter, rushing to their assignments, exquisitely dressed, elaborately coiffed, in snow white tabi and wooden sandals. The texture of their kimonos always slightly starched, the sleeves floating, like the wings of butterflies.

I saw women at work in factories. They wore blue denim kimonos, shabby from use but clean. They kneeled with their legs under them, at work with the same precision of gesture as their more glamorous counterparts. The hair was not lacquered or worked into rounded chignons, but neatly braided.

The modern emancipated Japanese women remained in Tokyo. During the rest of the trip the women I saw seemed to please the eye, to answer miraculously a need for a drink.

Their costumes bound them but their gestures remained light and airy, transcending the tightness of the obi. Their feet in the wooden sandals were as light as ballet dancers'.

In the fields, the peasant women at work presented the

same harmonious dress of coarse dark blue denim, uniform and soigné even when worn. The straw hat, the basket, were also uniform, and the women worked with such order in their alignment that they seemed like a beautifully designed group dance. I watched them pick weeds, in a row, on their knees, with baskets beside them, and they picked in rhythm, without deviations or fumblings. The women weeded gardens while the men took care of the trees or cleaned the ponds of surplus water lilies.

The softness, the all-enveloping attentiveness of the women—I thought of the Japanese films, in which this delicacy can turn into fierceness if challenged, in which they startle you with a dagger or even a sword at times. What kind of modern woman would emerge from the deep, masked, long-hidden Japanese woman of old? The whole mystery of the Japanese women lies behind their smooth faces, which rarely show age, except perhaps on peasant women battered by nature. But the smoothness remains from childhood far into maturity.

The thoughtfulness cannot be a mask, I concluded; it seems so natural, it seems like a genuine sensitiveness to others. It seems to come from identification and empathy.

Although my publishers were young—twenty-eight and twenty-nine years old—they did not introduce me to their wives. They were not invited to share in any of the dinners we had in restaurants or visits to the Noh plays and kabuki. To console myself I collected a large amount of novels, thinking I would then become more intimate with the feelings and thoughts of Japanese women. It was a woman, Lady Murasaki, who wrote the first diary in the year 900, and although it is a Proustian work of subtle and elaborate detail, although the feelings and thoughts of the personages at court are described, the woman herself remains an image. The modern works of women writers are not translated.

And the novels, as a whole, did not bring me any closer to the Japanese woman. The same element of selflessness enters into the novels. Very few of the women are dominant or self-assertive. There is a strong tendency to live according to the code, the mores, the religious or cultural rules. To live for a collective ideal. The one who breaks away is described as a monster of evil.

On one of the touring buses on the way to Kiushu, there was a young woman guide in a light blue uniform, with a small white cap and white gloves. She was in reality homely, but her expression radiated such aliveness, such responsiveness, and participation to the voyagers, such warmth and friendliness that she kept the mood of the travellers high through an arduous and difficult day. At each village the bus stopped at, she sang the folk song of the region. Her voice was clear and sweet like a child's, and yet it had a haunting quality like that of a wistful flute played in solitude. Through heat, through fatigue, through harassing travellers, she remained fresh, buoyant, light footed, carrying her modern burden of work as lightly as if it were a fan.

The children present a different mystery: the mystery of discipline and love dosed in such balance that they appear as the most spontaneous children I have ever seen, and at the same time the best behaved. They are lively, cheerful, charming, outgoing, expressive, and free, but their freedom never ends in sullenness or anarchy. I witnessed Japanese school children being guided through a museum, who came upon an American child of their own age. They surrounded him gaily, twittering and speaking the few words of English they knew. The American child looked sullen, suspicious, and withdrawn.

Through the gardens and the museums, they were responsive, curious. Their gaiety was continuous but contained. In Kyoto, during the Gion Festival, which lasts for several hours, the children were everywhere, but they did not disrupt the ceremony. The heat did not wilt them, the crowd did not dirty them, their clothes did not wrinkle. Had they learned so young to defeat slovenliness and ill-humor, to emerge fresh and gracious from the most wearing day? I thought of the gardens of Japan, the order, the stylization, the control of nature, so that they present only an aesthetically perfect image. Have the Japanese naturally achieved this miracle of aesthetic perfection? No weeds, no dead leaves, no disorder, no tangles, no withered flowers, no mud-splattered paths?

Such is my memory of women and children of Japan.

In Favor
of the
Sensitive
Man

This last year I spent most of my time with young women in colleges, young women doing their Ph.D.'s on my work. The talk about the diaries always led to private and intimate talks about their lives. I became aware that the ideals, fantasies, and desires of these women were going through a transition. Intelligent, gifted, participating in the creativity and activities of their time in history, they seem to have transcended the attraction for the conventional definition of a man.

They had learned to expose the purely macho type, his false masculinity, physical force, dexterity in games, arrogance, but more dangerous still, his lack of sensitivity. The hero of *Last Tango in Paris* repulsed them. The sadist, the man who humiliates woman, whose show of power is a façade. The so-called heroes, the stance of a Hemingway or a Mailer in writing, the false strength. All this was exposed, disposed of by these new women, too intelligent to be deceived, too wise and too proud to be subjected to this display of power which did not protect them (as former generations of women believed) but endangered their existence as individuals.

From *Playgirl*, September 1974.

The attraction shifted to the poet, the musician, the singer, the sensitive man they had studied with, to the natural, sincere man without stance or display, nonassertive, the one concerned with true values, not ambition, the one who hates war and greed, commercialism and political expediencies. A new type of man to match the new type of woman. They helped each other through college, they answered each other's poems, they wrote confessional and self-examining letters, they prized their relationship, they gave care to it, time, attention. They did not like impersonal sensuality. Both wanted to work at something they loved.

I met many couples who fitted this description. Neither one dominated. Each one worked at what he did best, shared labors, unobtrusively, without need to establish roles or boundaries. The characteristic trait was gentleness. There was no head of the house. There was no need to assert which one was the supplier of income. They had learned the subtle art of oscillation, which is human. Neither strength nor weakness is a fixed quality. We all have our days of strength and our days of weakness. They had learned rhythm, suppleness, relativity. Each had knowledge and special intuitions to contribute. There is no war of the sexes between these couples. There is no need to draw up contracts on the rules of marriage. Most of them do not feel the need to marry. Some want children and some do not. They are both aware of the function of dreams—not as symptoms of neurosis, but as guidance to our secret nature. They know that each is endowed with both masculine and feminine qualities.

A few of these young women displayed a new anxiety. It was as though having lived so long under the direct or indirect domination of man (setting the style of their life, the pattern, the duties) they had become accustomed to it, and now that it was gone, now that they were free to make

In Favor of the Sensitive Man

47

decisions, to be mobile, to speak their wishes, to direct their own lives, they felt like ships without rudders. I saw questions in their eyes. Was sensitivity felt as overgentle? Permissiveness as weakness? They missed authority, the very thing they had struggled to overcome. The old groove had functioned for so long. Women as dependents. A few women independent, but few in proportion to the dependent ones. The offer of total love was unusual. A love without egocentricity, without exigencies, without moral strictures. A love which did not define the duties of women (you must do this and that, you must help me with my work, you must entertain and further my career).

A love which was almost a twinship. No potentates, no dictators. Strange. It was new. It was a new country. You cannot have independence and dependence. You can alternate them equally, and then both can grow, unhampered, without obstacles. This sensitive man is aware of woman's needs. He seeks to let her be. But sometimes women do not recognize that the elements they are missing are those which thwarted woman's expansion, her testing of her gifts, her mobility, her development. They mistake sensitivity for weakness. Perhaps because the sensitive man lacks the aggressiveness of the macho man (which sends him hurtling through business and politics at tragic cost to family and personal relationships).

I met a young man, who although the head of a business by inheritance, did not expect his wife to serve the company, to entertain people not attractive to her, to assist in his contacts. She was free to pursue her own interests, which lay in psychology and training welfare workers. She became anxious that the two different sets of friends, his business associates and her psychologists, would create totally separate lives and estrange them. It took her a while to observe that her psychological experiences were serving his interests in another way. He was learning to handle those who worked for him in a more humanistic way. When an employee was found cheating while pumping the company's gas to the other employees, he called him in and obtained his life history. He discovered the reason for the cheating (high hospital bills for a child) and remedied it instead of firing him, thus winning a loyal employee from then on. The couple's interests, which seemed at first divergent, became interdependent.

Another couple decided that, both being writers, one would teach one year and leave the other free to write, and the other would take on teaching the next year. The husband was already a fairly well known writer. The wife had only published poems in magazines but was preparing a book of criticism. It was her turn to teach. He found himself considered a faculty member's husband and was asked at parties, "Do you also write?" The situation could have caused friction. The wife remedied it by having reprinted in the school paper a review of her husband's last novel, which established his standing.

Young women are engaging in political action when young men are withdrawing because of disillusionment. And the new woman is winning new battles. The fact that certain laws were changed renewed the faith of the new man. Women in politics are still at the stage of David and Goliath. They believe in the effect of a single stone! Their faith is invigorating when they and their husbands have sympathetic vibes, as they call it.

The old situation of the man obsessed with business, whose life was shortened by stress, and whose life ended at retirement, was reversed by a young wife who encouraged his hobby, painting, so that he retired early to enjoy art and travel.

In these situations the art of coordination manifests itself rather than the immature emphasis on irreconcilable differences. With maturity comes the sense that activities are interrelated and nourish one another.

Another source of bewilderment for the new woman is that many of the new men do not have the old ambitions. They do not want to spend their lives in the pursuit of a fortune. They want to travel while they are young, live in the present. I met them hitchhiking in Greece, Spain, Italy, France. They were living entirely in the present and accepting the hardships for the sake of the present adventures. One young woman felt physically unfit for the difficulties and carried a lot of vitamins in her one and only pack. She told me: "At first he made fun of me, but then he understood I was not sure I could take the trip physically, and he became as protective as possible. If I had married a conventional man, his concept of protection would have been to keep me home. I would not have enjoyed all these marvels I have discovered with David, who challenged my strength and made me stronger for it." Neither one thought of surrendering the dream of travel while young.

One of the most frequent questions young women ask me is: How can a woman create a life of her own, an atmosphere of her own when her husband's profession dictates their lifestyle? If he is a doctor, a lawyer, a psychologist, a teacher, the place they live in, the demands of the neighbors, all set the pattern of life.

Judy Chicago, the well-known painter and teacher, made a study of women painters and found that, whereas the men painters all had studios separate from the house, the women did not, and painted either in the kitchen or some spare room. But many young women have taken literally Virginia Woolf's *A Room of One's Own* and rented studios away from the family. One couple who lived in a one-room house set up a tent on the terrace for the wife's writing activities. The very feeling of "going to work," the physical act of detachment, the sense of value given to the work by isolating it, became a stimulant and a help. To create another life, they found, was not a breaking away or separating. It is striking that for woman any break or separation carries with it an aura of loss, as if the symbolic umbilical cord still affected all her emotional life and each act were a threat to unity and ties.

This fear is in women, not in men, but it was learned from men. Men, led by their ambitions, did separate from their families, were less present for the children, were absorbed, submerged by their professions. But this happened to men and does not necessarily have to happen to women. The unbroken tie lies in the feelings. It is not the hours spent with husband or children, but the quality and completeness of the presence. Man is often physically present and mentally preoccupied. Woman is more capable of turning away from her work to give full attention to a weary husband or a child's scratched finger.

If women have witnessed the father "going away" because of his work, they will retain anxiety about their own "going away" to meetings, conferences, lectures, or other professional commitments.

For the new woman and the new man, the art of connecting and relating separate interests will be a challenge. If women today do not want a nonexistent husband married to Big Business, they will accept a simpler form of life to have the enjoyment of a husband whose life blood has not been sucked by big companies. I see the new woman shedding many luxuries. I love to see them, simply dressed, relaxed, natural, playing no roles. For the transitional stage was woman's delicate problem: how to pass from being submerged and losing her identity in a relationship, how to learn to merge without loss of self. The new man is helping by his willingness to change too, from rigidities to suppleness, from tightness to openness, from uncomfortable roles to the relaxation of no roles.

One young woman was offered a temporary teaching job away from home. The couple had no children. The young husband said: "Go ahead if that is what you want to do." If he had opposed the plan, which added to her teaching credits, she would have resented it. But because he let her go, she felt he did not love her deeply enough to hold on to her. She left with a feeling of being deserted, while he felt her leaving also as a desertion. These feelings lay below the conscious acceptance. The four months' separation might have caused a break. But the difference is that they were willing to discuss these feelings, to laugh at their ambivalence and contradictions.

If in the unconscious there still lie reactions we cannot control, at least we can prevent them from doing harm to the present situation. If both were unconsciously susceptible to the fear of being deserted, they had to find a way to grow independent from a childhood pattern. Otherwise, enslaved by childhood fears, neither one could move from the house. In exposing them they were able to laugh at the inconsistency of wanting freedom and yet wanting the other to hold on.

Very often in the emerging new woman, the assertion of differences carries too heavy an indication of dissonances, disharmony, but it is a matter of finding the relationships, as we are finding the relationship between art and science, science and psychology, religion and science. It is not similarities that create harmony, but the art of fusing various elements that enrich life. Professional activities tend to demand almost too much concentration; this becomes a narrowing of experience for each one. The infusion of new currents of thoughts, stretching the range of interests, is beneficial to both men and women.

Perhaps some new women and new men fear adventure and change. The life of Margaret Mead indicates that she sought a man with the same passionate devotion to anthropology, but the result was that her husband studied the legends, the myths of the tribe, and she was left to study childbirth and the raising of children. So a common interest does not necessarily mean equality.

All of us carry seeds of anxieties left from childhood, but the determination to live with others in close and loving harmony can overcome all the obstacles, provided we have learned to *integrate the differences.*

Watching these young couples and how they resolve the problems of new attitudes, new consciousness, I feel we might be approaching a humanistic era in which differences and inequalities may be resolved without war.

Yoko Ono proposed the "feminization of society. The use of feminine tendencies as a positive force to change the world . . . We can evolve rather than revolt."

The empathy these new men show woman is born of their acceptance of their own emotional, intuitive, sensory, and humanistic approach to relationships. They allow themselves to weep (men never wept), to show vulnerability, to expose their fantasies, share their inmost selves. Some women are baffled by the new regime. They have not yet recognized that to have empathy one must to some extent feel what the other feels. That means that if woman is to assert her creativity or her gifts, man has to assert his own crucial dislike of what was expected of him in the past.

The new type of young man I have met is exceptionally fitted for the new woman, but she is not yet totally appreciative of his tenderness, his growing proximity to woman, his attitude of twinship rather than differentiation. People who once lived under a dictatorship often are at a loss to govern themselves. This loss is a transitional one: It may mean the beginning of a totally new life and freedom. The man is there. He is an equal. He treats you like an equal. In moments of uncertainty you can still discuss problems with him you could not have talked about twenty years ago. Do not, I say to today's women, please do not mistake sensitivity for weakness. This was the mistake which almost doomed our culture. Violence was mistaken for power, the misuse of power for strength. The subjection is still true in films, in the theater, in the media. I wanted the hero of *Last Tango in Paris* to die immediately. He was only destroyed at the end! The time span of a film. Will it take women as long to recognize sadism, arrogance, tyranny, reflected so painfully in the world outside, in war and political corruption? Let us start the new regime of honesty, of trust, abolishment of false roles in our personal relationships, and it will eventually affect the world's history as well as women's development.

Writing,
Music, and
Films

On Truth
and Reality

There are books which we read early in life, which sink into our consciousness and seem to disappear without leaving a trace. And then one day we find, in some summing-up of our life and our attitudes towards experience, that their influence has been enormous. Such a book is *Truth and Reality*, by Otto Rank, which I read in my early thirties. Its French title is *La Volonté du Bonheur* (*The Will to Happiness*). I read every word, and it must have penetrated so very deeply to a place where I no longer was consciously aware of, into the depths of my subconscious. It was not an intellectual experience for me, but a deeply emotional one. So the meaning of this book, its guiding principles, sank into my unconscious and I did not read it again until, thanks to Virginia Robinson and Anita Faatz, I rediscovered it and found that my whole life as a woman artist had been influenced by it, and proved its wisdom.

I must have based myself on its principles. Dr. Rank stressed several goals, and I will refer later to how much more difficult it was for a woman to achieve them than for

A lecture given at the meeting of The Otto Rank Association, in Doylestown, Pennsylvania, 28 October 1972; first published in the *Journal of the Otto Rank Association*, June 1973.

a man. In his book he speaks constantly about the "creative will." I even forgot that expression and used instead my own, which is stubbornness. I said very often that I was more stubborn than other writers. I would not give up, I have never given up, but I didn't call it creative will. It is a beautiful phrase.

This creative will sometimes manifests itself very early in life. At the age of nine I was in danger of losing my life. A doctor made a mistaken diagnosis and said I had tuberculosis of the hip and would never walk again. My instant reaction was to ask for pencil and paper and begin to make written portraits of my whole family, to write poems. I even put on the front page of these notes "Member of the French Academy," which to me seemed the highest honor awarded to a writer. This is an attitude of defiance, it is actually the refusal to despair, the refusal to bow down to the human condition, human sorrows, human handicaps. Last-minute surgery saved my life. But this is where the writing began. It was a dramatization of the artist's solution to the obstacles of life. All my life I have talked and written a great deal about the artist. It was often misunderstood as cultist, excluding nonartists and uncreative people, but this was not so. I love nonartists as well, but for me the artist simply means one who can transform ordinary life into a beautiful creation with his craft. But I did not mean creation strictly applied only to the arts, I meant creation in life, the creation of a child, a garden, a house, a dress. I was referring to creativity in all its aspects. Not only the actual products of art, but the faculty for healing, consoling, raising the level of life, transforming it by our own efforts. I was talking about the creative will, which Dr. Rank opposed to neurosis as our salvation. When I went to see him (I was twenty-eight years old or so) I felt oppressed and actually trapped by my human commitments, by the human condition particularly applied to woman with her training for devotion, service, loyalty to her personal world. I started with the usual handicaps which I share with so many: the broken home, uprooting to a strange country whose language I did not know. Everything contributed to create an alienated child. I found it extremely difficult to enter the flow of life, difficult and painful because there was always the double struggle which Dr. Rank describes in *Truth and Reality*: the conflict between being different and wanting to be close to others. I felt different but I longed for friendship and love. The struggle to maintain my difference was accentuated by the cultural contrasts and uprooting, the problem of language. I was holding on to the values I had been taught, yet I wanted to be admitted to the adopted culture. I finally learned the language, and actually fell in love with English. But the two cultures worked against my sense of unity, two cultures which were opposites, the European and the American.

When I went to see Dr. Rank, instead of tackling the immediate problems, the difficulties in my relationships, the conflicts of cultures, the conflicts between fiction writer and diarist, between woman and writer, he instantly realized the seriousness of my existence as a writer. He focussed on the strongest element in my divided and chaotic self. No matter what disintegrating influences I was experiencing, the writing was the act of wholeness. What he did was to practice his own philosophy, which was to disregard the negativities we usually bring to the therapist and focus on the most positive element in my nature, which was the stubborn concern with writing. I was amazed that he left aside the human problems. Later I realized what a stroke of genius this was. First of all he asked me to put my diary down on his table, in other words to give it up as a hiding

place, a place for secrets, for a separate existence. So I
would share everything with him. I realized later he had
shifted the whole problem of human life to the problem of
the creative will, and that he was counting on this creative
will to find its own solutions. He was challenging my creative will, and having strengthened that, I began to alter
my personal life. The change came from within; it was a
force which could solve conflicts and dualities. That is why
I give the artist such importance, because he possesses this
power from the beginning. Even in the darkest periods of
social history, outer events would be changed if we had a
center. It is only in the private world that we can learn
to alchemize the ugly, the terrible, the horrors of war, the
evils and cruelties of man, into a new kind of human being.
I do not say turn away or escape. We cannot turn away
from social history, because it is necessary to maintain our
responsibilities to society, but we need to create a center of
strength and resistance to disappointments and failures in
outward events. Today I am working for causes which I
consider worthwhile, but that is in the world of action, and
the world from which we draw our wisdom, our lucidities,
our power to act, our courage, is in this other world which is
not an escape but a laboratory of the soul. It is this inner
world Dr. Rank was eager to see us create, and for that he
had to deliver us from the sense of guilt, inbred in us, towards individual growth. In *Truth and Reality* he does say
that the culture tries to make us feel that the active individual is really endangering the growth of his fellow men. And I
had this problem, in common with so many students today.
When I talked about individual growth in order to have
something to contribute to the collective, they thought I
meant to turn away and take refuge in an ivory tower. For
me it was the place where I did my most difficult spiritual
work, where I practiced the confrontation of psychological

obstacles, in order to be able to act and live in the world without despair and loss of faith. It was the place where I reconstructed what the outer world disintegrated. Because it is just as important to live outside of history as it is to live within it. Because history is only an aggregate of personal hostilities, personal prejudices, personal blindness and irrationality, there are times when we have to live against it. Our American culture made a virtue of our living only as extroverts. We discouraged the inner journey, the quest for a center, and so we lost our center and had to find it again.

Someone asked me the other day, Are we ever going to reach a time when we don't need therapy? I answered, Not until we cease to be in trouble for lack of a center. Dr. Rank talked about this and mentioned that guilt accompanies every act of will—creative will or the assertion of our personal will. He knew the extent of our guilt. The artist knows it. It was proved very often in the history of artists' lives. They often expressed the need to justify their work, to justify their concentration and even obsession with it.

Now, in the woman this problem is far deeper, because the guilt which afflicts woman is deeper than man's. Man is expected to achieve. He is expected to become the finest doctor, the finest lawyer, the finest teacher, etc. Whatever he does is expected of him by society, and he is delivered of guilt when he produces. But woman was trained to give first place to her personal commitments—home and children and husband or family—she was encumbered with duties which absorbed all her energies, and the very concept of love was united to the concept of care and nurturing, whether physical or symbolic. When she reduced the hours of devotion and gave her energies to other interests, she felt a double guilt. She was made aware that she was failing in her personal responsibilities, and her other achievements were severely undervalued by the culture. So the guilt is much deeper in woman and becomes in many cases the roots of her neurosis or even pathology.

Then there is another guilt peculiar to women. Our culture stresses rivalry, competition, as a legitimate motivation. But any advancement achieved by woman was considered competitive even when it was not motivated by it. In the early days when I was a young woman, I stated that I would rather be the wife of an artist than to be one myself. It was a way of avoiding conflict. I would live vicariously through the man, I would be all the artist needed—muse, assistant, the protective, nurturing mother. In my twenties this role seemed more comfortable. It was only when I met Dr. Rank that I realized I had my own work to do. When we live vicariously we expect the other to do our work, and we are disappointed if he does his own, diverging from our wishes. But before meeting Dr. Rank I conceived of growth as a big tree overshadowing other trees, endangering their flowering by absorbing all the light. I wanted to grow but I didn't want that to interfere with anybody else's growth. I must have conceived of growth as ultimately a giant redwood tree. I have never heard of a male artist concerned about the effect of his growth and expansion on his family. We accept the fact that his work justifies all sacrifices. But woman does not feel this is enough of a justification.

As a woman I was fully aware that it was my personal world which was the source of my strength and my psychic energy. The creation of a perfect personal world was the root of my inspiration. So woman is concerned with not losing this center, which she knows the value of. Just as the deep-sea diver carries a tank of oxygen, we have to carry the kernel of our individual growth with us into the world in order to withstand the pressures, the shattering pressures of outer experiences. But I never lost sight of their interdependence, and now I find in Dr. Rank the following statement: "Whatever we achieve inwardly will change outer reality."

According to American culture I spent many years doing what is defined as an egocentric work, an introspective and subjective work, a selfish work. I was keeping a diary which kept me in contact with my deepest self, which was a mirror reflecting my growth or the pauses in this growth, as well as making me attentive to the growth of those around me. I continued to be dependent on the therapist ever so many years because he delivered me from cultural guilt and projected me into new cycles. Each cycle was a different drama. The first one was the relation to the missing father, the second cycle was the relation to the mother from whom I took the concept of female sacrifice, the third was the assertion of my own creative will. A final, a synthesizing analysis by a woman finally brought me to a harmony among all the parts of myself. But it was only when the diaries were published and their usefulness to others was established that I became entirely free of guilt. Which proves Dr. Rank's point again that whatever we achieve is ultimately our gift to the community and to the collective life. Dr. Rank suspected, as I do, that group activities weaken our will. They may be a solace to loneliness, but they do not foster the individual creative will. It is necessary to establish this first before engaging in group activities. For Dr. Rank the supreme achievement was this creative will which could resist brain washing of various kinds. So often in women's groups I saw individuals bring to the group only personal problems, neurotic problems which should have been taken to therapy, for the group is not trained to solve such problems. We should not bring to the collective an unfinished, distressed, chaotic, confused, sick, or hurt self.

At this time I would like to have you talk with me.

There's a word I love very much, *furrawn*, which is from the Welsh. It means a kind of talk that creates intimacy. I would like to know if you have any questions to ask me or things to tell me in relation to this creative will, which was Rank's great contribution to the psychology of woman.

QUESTIONER: What do you think the group can do for us?
ANAÏS NIN: If you have a clear idea of what the problem is, the group may help in the solution of it, but we do not always have a clear idea of what is disturbing us. I think the group can make women feel less lonely, and they can become aware that many problems are similar. The strength it gives is the same as that given by solid friendships, but I do not think the group can give self-awareness or strength in any permanent form.

Q: Would you comment briefly on the current women writers. I can only think of two of them, Joan Didion and Sylvia Plath. I have read reviews of their books and once I read the reviews I was reluctant to read what they wrote.

AN: It is possible you felt as I do, that writers who write only about despair, hopelessness, destructiveness, do not attract you. I am not speaking in terms of literature. That is why I was not attracted to the book by Simone de Beauvoir on aging. I felt that she had accepted chronological age whereas there is no generalization about age. Age is psychic too. Some people read to confirm their own hopelessness. Others read to be rescued from it.

Q: Would you comment further on the lifesaving force and the revitalization process within the ivory tower?

AN: One answer lies in Otto Rank's *Truth and Reality*. That is the process by which we create ourselves. The other lies in therapy. Therapy is not only a healing of neurosis. It is a lesson on how to grow, how to overcome the obstacles to our growth. Experiences tend to alienate us. We close up defensively. To protect ourselves from pain, we dull our responses. Psychology removes the scars, the fears, the rigidities which prevent us from expanding. It is a revivifying process.

The Story
of My
Printing
Press

In the 1940s, two of my books, *Winter of Artifice* and *Under a Glass Bell,* were rejected by American publishers. *Winter of Artifice* had been published in France, in English, and had been praised by Rebecca West, Henry Miller, Lawrence Durrell, Kay Boyle, and Stuart Gilbert. Both books were considered uncommercial. I want writers to know where they stand in relation to such verdicts from commercial publishers, and to offer a solution which is still effective today. I am thinking of writers who are the equivalent of researchers in science, whose appeal does not elicit immediate gain.

I did not accept the verdict and decided to print my own books. For seventy-five dollars I bought a second-hand press. It was foot-powered like the old sewing machines, and one had to press the treadle very hard to develop sufficient power to turn the wheel.

Frances Steloff, who owned the Gotham Book Mart in New York, loaned me one hundred dollars for the enterprise, and Thurema Sokol loaned me another hundred. I bought type for a hundred dollars, used orange crates for shelves, and bought paper remnants, which is like buying

From the *Publish-It-Yourself Handbook*, Pushcart, 1973.

remnants of materials to make a dress. Some of this paper was quite beautiful, left over from de luxe editions. A friend, Gonzalo More, helped me. He had a gift for designing books. I learned to set type, and he ran the machine. We learned printing from library books, which gave rise to comical accidents. For example, the book said, "oil the rollers," so we oiled the entire rollers including the rubber part, and wondered why we could not print for a week.

James Cooney, of *Phoenix* magazine, gave us helpful technical advice. Our lack of knowledge of printed English also led to such errors as my own (now-famous) word separation in *Winter of Artifice:* "lo-ve." But more important than anything else, setting each letter by hand taught me economy of style. After living with a page for a whole day, I could detect the superfluous words. At the end of each line I thought, is this word, is this phrase, absolutely necessary?

It was hard work, patient work, to typeset prose, to lock the tray, to carry the heavy lead tray to the machine, to run the machine itself, which had to be inked by hand, to set the copper plates (for the illustrations) on inch-thick wood supports in order to print them. Printing copper plates meant inking each plate separately, cleaning it after one printing, and starting the process over again. It took me months to typeset *Under a Glass Bell* and *Winter of Artifice.* Then there were the printed pages to be placed between blotters and later cut, gathered into signatures, and put together for the binder. Then the type had to be redistributed in the boxes.

We had problems finding a bookbinder willing to take on such small editions and to accept the unconventional shape of the books.

Frances Steloff agreed to distribute them and gave me an autograph party at the Gotham Book Mart. The completed books were beautiful and have now become collector's items.

The first printing of *Winter of Artifice* was three hundred copies, and one publisher I met at a party exclaimed: "I don't know how you managed to become so well known with only three hundred books."

Under a Glass Bell was given to Edmund Wilson by Frances Steloff. He reviewed it favorably in the *New Yorker,* and immediately all the publishers were ready to reprint both books in commercial editions.

We did not use the word "underground" then, but this tiny press and word of mouth enabled my writing to be discovered. The only handicap was that newspapers and magazines took no notice of books by small presses, and it was almost impossible to obtain a review. Edmund Wilson's review was an exception. It launched me. I owe him that and am only sorry that his acceptance did not extend to the rest of my work.

I had to reprint both books with a loan from Samuel Goldberg, the lawyer.

Someone thought I should send the story of the press to the *Reader's Digest.* The *Digest's* response was that if I had to print the books myself, they must be bad. Many people still believe that, and for many years there was a suspicion that my difficulties with publishers indicated a doubtful quality in my work. A year before the publication of the diary, a Harvard student wrote in the *Harvard Advocate* that the silence of critics and the indifference of commercial publishers must necessarily mean the work was flawed.

A three-hundred-copy edition of *Winter of Artifice,* press, type, and bookbinding cost four hundred dollars. The books sold for three dollars. I printed announcements and circularized friends and acquaintances. The entire edition of both books was sold out.

But the physical work was so overwhelming that it interfered with my writing. This is the only reason I accepted the offer of a commercial publisher and surrendered the press. Otherwise I would have liked to continue with my own press, controlling both the content and design of the books.

I regretted giving up the press, for with the commercial publishers my troubles began. Then, as today, they wanted quick and large returns. This gamble for quick returns has nothing whatever to do with the deeper needs of the public, nor can a publisher's selection of a book be considered as representative of the people's choice. The impetus starts with the belief of the publisher, who backs his choice with advertising disguised as literary judgment. Thus books are imposed on the public like any other commercial product. In my case the illogical attitude of publishers was clear. They took me on as a prestige writer, but a prestige writer does not rate publicity, and therefore sales were modest. Five thousand copies of commercially published *Ladders to Fire* was not enough.

The universal quality in good writing, which publishers claim to recognize, is impossible to define. My books, which were not supposed to have this universal quality, were nevertheless bought and read by all kinds of people.

Today, instead of feeling embittered by the opposition of publishers, I am happy they opposed me, for the press gave me independence and confidence. I felt in direct contact with my public, and it was enough to sustain me through the following years. My early dealings with commercial publishers ended in disaster. They were not satisfied with the immediate sales, and neither the publishers nor the bookstores were interested in long-range sales. But fortunately, I found Alan Swallow in Denver, Colorado, a self-made and independent publisher who had started with a press in his garage. He adopted what he called his "maverick writers." He kept all my books in print, was content with simply earning a living, and our common struggles created a strong bond. He had the same problems with distribution and reviewing I had known, and we helped each other. He lived long enough to see the beginning of my popularity, the success of the diaries, to see the books he kept alive taught in universities. I am writing his story in Volume Six of the diary.

What this story implies is that commercial publishers, being large corporate establishments, should sustain explorative and experimental writers, just as business sustains researchers, and not expect huge, immediate gains from them. They herald new attitudes, new consciousness, new evolutions in the taste and minds of people. They are the researchers who sustain the industry. Today my work is in harmony with the new values, the new search and state of mind of the young. This synchronism is one nobody could have foreseen, except by remaining open-minded to innovation and pioneering.

Novelist
on Stage

D. H. Lawrence's complete dramaturgic output—eight full-
length plays and two fragments, written at various points
in his literary career, from 1909 onward—has now been
published in a single volume. While the book mysteriously
lacks introductory comment of any sort, and while Lawrence is not widely recognized for his stagecraft (only a few
of the plays ever having been produced), the collection is
interesting for the light it sheds on Lawrence's efforts to
express his ideas in a different medium.

The plays will appeal to those who are mystified by Lawrence's daring and unique attempt to crack the surface of
naturalism in his novels, to find a way to release emotions,
instincts, intuitions, to find a special language of the senses.
For the dramatic form, with its severe limitations on lyric
expression, would not seem suited to Lawrence's aims.

In his plays, which range from situation comedy to real-
ism, Lawrence respects the need for action and dialogue—
faithfulness to what is manifested on the surface and directly expressed. Absent are deep exploration of motivations
and emotional ambivalences. Direct, simple, almost classical, and free of admixture, these plays remind one of the

A review of *The Complete Plays of D. H. Lawrence*, in *The New York Times Book Review*, 10 April 1966.

perfect rendering of the illusion of reality by the Moscow Art Theater. Lawrence does not strive for dénouements, for tension; he is content to present a lifelike portrait of instants. He makes no attempt to break with conventions of the theater, as he did with those of the novel.

His favorite themes, similar to the themes of his novels, are reduced to extreme artlessness. At times his faithfulness to ordinary dialogue is extreme, as in *The Daughter-in-Law*, where he supplies a shorthand colloquialism for the spoken dialect which is to me almost unreadable. He records the atmosphere of poverty. He is concerned with the simple patterns of daily life which help to contain outbreaks of emotion. He endows these patterns with ritualistic meaning that conveys inner states of mind. The serving of food, the very descriptions of food itself, laundering, ironing, folding sheets, baking bread, making beds, lighting lamps or candles, are anchors and roots to prevent emotional explosions.

His poetic moments are sensitive and unadorned. In *The Widowing of Mrs. Holroyd*, Mrs. Holroyd, while her husband is drinking at the pub, is visited by Blackmore, the electrician working around a mine who describes himself as a gentleman: "ours is gentlemen's work."

She puts her two palms on the table and leans back. He draws near to her, dropping his head.

BLACKMORE: Look here! (*He has put his hand on the table near hers.*)

MRS. HOLROYD: Yes, I know you've got nice hands—but you needn't be vain of them.

BLACKMORE: No—it's not that— But don't they seem— (*He glances swiftly at her; she turns her head aside; he laughs nervously.*)—they sort of go well with one another. (*He laughs again.*)

MRS. HOLROYD: They *do*, rather—."

This is a key moment in the play, for the attraction between them dramatized by this quiet scene has its preparation and consequences. Blackmore is aware that Mrs. Holroyd suffers from her husband's drinking—that he brutalizes the family when he returns from his drinking sprees and has humiliated her by bringing prostitutes to his home. Mrs. Holroyd has wished for his death, to be free of him. She confesses this to Blackmore. But when her husband dies in a mine accident she is distraught; she feels that it is her wish which caused his death. She says despairingly, "I never loved you enough."

In *The Married Man* Lawrence attempts light comedy and is less successful. He deals with complicated philandering, but adds little touches typical of his writing: "I should think it would be the easiest thing in life to write a poem about a couch. I never see a couch but my heart moves to poetry. The very buttons must be full of echoes."

All the plays foreshadow the series of films made so much later about working classes in England: the moods for Tony Richardson's *The Loneliness of the Long Distance Runner* and Karel Reisz's *Saturday Night and Sunday Morning*; inarticulate tenderness; frustrated ambitions; atmospheres of limitation and greyness.

In *The Daughter-in-Law* a husband is unfaithful, the wife leaves him, but then returns to find her husband has been wounded in a strike. They rediscover the depth of their love for each other.

In *Touch and Go* Lawrence tackles a social theme, and shows that he was able as early as 1920 to foresee that the struggle of labor against capital would be thwarted not by objective factors (whether or not the demands were fair) but by the personal, irrational, subjective resistance of individuals.

A *Collier's Friday Night*, which parallels *Sons and Lovers*, is probably the most moving of all the plays. The father drinks and is brutal, the mother feels superior to him and has transferred her love to her son. She is jealous of her son's interest in a young girl, Maggie, and when he goes to visit her she cannot sleep until he returns safely home. When her son tries to explain that there are different kinds of love, that there are things he can talk about with Maggie which he cannot talk about with her, she can only reproach him for not loving her more than anyone else. The play ends with a full expression of their love, an overwhelming tenderness. "There is in their tone a dangerous gentleness—so much gentleness that the safe reserve of their soul is broken."

It is this reserve (which is rarely broken in the plays) which makes them less revealing of other dimensions than are the novels, where Lawrence proved himself a speleologist of the unconscious. He penetrated realms people feared and did not acknowledge. He portrayed ambivalences, dualities, and instinctive, intuitive states. He allowed his characters moments of desperation, loss of control, blind impulsiveness. Those who were not at ease with these explorations, who do not wish to witness any outbreaks of the irrational in the pattern of harmonious tradition, will prefer the plays, with their detachment and linear organization.

Out of the Labyrinth: An Interview

EAST WEST JOURNAL: At what point in your life did you recognize your own commitment as a writer?

ANAÏS NIN: Very early, because of a mistaken diagnosis when I was nine years old that I wouldn't walk. I immediately took to writing, and then after that of course I began the diary at eleven.

EWJ: Did you read a great deal as a child?

AN: Yes, voraciously.

EWJ: In the diaries you frequently mention Marcel Proust. Has his work influenced your writing?

AN: Proust was very important; he was the first one to show me how to break down the chronology (which I never like) and to follow the dictates and intuitions of memory, of feeling memory, so that he only wrote things when he felt them, no matter when it happened. And of course this element became very strong in my work. But there were also other influences. I wanted to write a poetic novel, and for that I chose models like Giraudoux, Pierre-Jean Jouve, and also Djuna Barnes, an American writer and author of *Nightwood*. Later on it was D. H. Lawrence. Lawrence

An interview by Jody Hoy, in the *East West Journal*, August 1974.

showed me the way to find a language for emotion, for instinct, for ambivalence, for intuition.

EWJ: Do you identify yourself now as an American writer?

AN: I'm really writing for America and in English, but I would like to go beyond that. I can't say I'm an American writer, although I'm identified with the new consciousness. I prefer to think of myself in more universal or international terms, particularly as I partake of two cultures. On the other hand, many foreign-born writers have been incorporated into the mainstream of American literature, yet Americans still say "foreign-born Nabokov," and in my case, "Paris-born Anaïs."

EWJ: Is the cross-cultural background to which you refer a possible source of the inner density and flow in your work?

AN: I always felt the inner quality resulted from the trauma of being uprooted and of losing my father, then of realizing I had to build an inner world which would withstand destruction. The child who is uprooted begins to recognize that what he builds within himself is what will endure, what will withstand shattering experiences.

EWJ: Your works often evoke symphonic form. Do you feel that music has influenced your writing?

AN: Very strongly. I even said as directly as that in the diary that my ideal would be a page of writing which would be like a page of music. There must be a language, a way of expressing things, which bypasses the intellect and goes straight to the emotions. I wanted to evoke the same reaction to writing that I have to music.

EWJ: I'm interested in the creative process itself, how you move from the interior vision to its exteriorization in literature.

AN: My concern was for exterior reality as holding a secret of a metaphor. I would never describe the city or the ragpickers or a person without looking for the inner meaning.

Writing, Music, and Films

When you are concerned with the metaphysical meaning, everything becomes transparent. I never described a city for its own sake but immediately had to find what its spiritual qualities were. Its symbolic value is what makes it seem transparent, people would even say dreamlike, but that wasn't what it was.

EWJ: What place would you assign to the dream in your works, and what significance to the constancy of flow and communication between the conscious and the unconscious?

AN: Unfortunately, we tend to separate everything. We separate the body and soul. We separate the dream from our daily life. What I found in psychology was the inter-relationship between them, and I wanted to keep those passageways open, to be able to move from one dimension to the other, not to divide them even, so that they were really one. The next step was carrying it into the novel, always starting the novel with a dream, having that dream be the theme of the novel to be developed, understood, and fulfilled if possible at the end in order to be able to move on to the next experience.

EWJ: How do you explain the almost universal identification of your women readers with the characters in your novels?

AN: I believe that what unites us universally is our emotions, our feelings in the face of experience, and not necessarily the actual experiences themselves. The facts were different, but readers felt the same way towards a father even if the father was different. So I think unwittingly I must have gone so deep inside what Ira Progoff calls the "personal well" that I touched the water at a level where it connected all the wells together.

EWJ: Is part of your uniqueness as a writer due to the fact that you venture into realms which relate specifically to woman's situation and experience?

AN: My own subjective attitude towards reality was all I really knew, what I could see and feel. I read a great deal, but I didn't imitate men writers. I wanted to tell what I saw. So it came out a woman's vision of the universe, a highly personal vision. I wanted to translate man to woman and woman to man. I didn't want to lose contact with the language of man, but I knew that there was a distinction of levels.

EWJ: Among your works is there one which, from your own point of view, is the best written?

AN: I could never rewrite the short stories. I couldn't add one word to the short stories in *Under a Glass Bell*. I couldn't change anything in *Collages*.

EWJ: Do you use a different artistic yardstick or measure for the diaries?

AN: In writing the diary, I tried to overlook, to forget all procedures of writing. I wanted to make no demands on myself as to whether I'd written it well or not well. I wanted to shed all that, and I succeeded because I felt it would never be read.

EWJ: The diaries were originally not intended to be published?

AN: No.

EWJ: How did they come to be published?

AN: Occasionally I would have a desire to share a part of the diary, or I would write something I was proud of. I did let some people read a part here and there; for example, I let Henry Miller read his portrait. So, there was a little bit of sharing. But feeling that I could solve the problems of editing a diary didn't come till much later, when as a practiced novelist I felt I could handle the problem of editing. Also, I had to handle the psychological problem of being open, the fear of exposing myself. I had a terrifying dream that I opened my front door and was struck by mortal radiation. But then the opposite happened. I overcame that, I overcame the editing problems and then, of course, I was open.

EWJ: Do you use the diary as a resource for the novels and short stories?

AN: Yes, it's really a notebook. Sometimes if I keep writing about a person who interests me, after a while I have a cumulative portrait. We don't think of our friends in that way, we see them a little bit here and a little bit there. Suddenly I see a total person, then I write the story.

EWJ: Has your exceptional beauty been an asset or a disadvantage?

AN: Sometimes it was an asset when you could charm a critic, and sometimes it really stood in the way. Even in women the feeling persists that beauty means there isn't anything inside. I never believed in mine, so that made it very simple.

EWJ: In the diaries, you speak with great attachment of your home in Louveciennes. Do you consider environment an extension of personality in the same way that clothing constitutes a symbolic extension of character in your novels?

AN: Yes. I also believe we need to change our environment as we evolve. I know the history of Louveciennes ended at a certain time. Looking back on it, it was the right time. Even though it's painful and you are not necessarily aware when you're finished with a certain experience, you do know, something propels you out. I have been propelled out of several homes. When a certain cycle ends, the house itself becomes dead. I think these are reflections of where we are at the moment.

EWJ: In your writings you express a profound belief in the human capacity to grow beyond neurosis. What is the source of your optimism?

AN: I never thought about the source. I always felt that

impulse in myself, the way plants have an impulse to grow. I believe what happens are accidental interferences and blockages. We all have that impulse but then it gets damaged occasionally. It's in children, isn't it? They use their strengths, their skills, and explore everything, all possibilities. I believe that we can take notice of the damage which most of us sustain somewhere along the line and we can overcome the damage. We all have interferences, discouragements, and traumatic experiences. I have met young writers who have stopped at the first rejection notice. So it's a question of how much we are willing to struggle in order to overcome the impediments.

EWJ: Would you say that one of the major themes in your works is the conflict between woman's role as a dependent and loving being and the artist's drive toward transcendence?

AN: Yes, I think that is a very great conflict. The creative will pushes you in one direction while you have guilt about using time and energy which is supposed to be devoted to your personal life. It hasn't been a problem for man because the culture incites him to produce, he wants to be obsessed with his work, he is blessed for it. But woman has really been told that the primary concern is her personal life, she hasn't been encouraged to create; in her case it is accidental phenomena.

EWJ: In terms of the growth impulse or process, do you believe that we evolve out of childhood, that we grow away from childhood and leave it behind, or do we, as we grow, effect a reunion with a primary self before trauma? Is growth a linear process of moving away or a circular process of return to an essential self?

AN: I would agree with you that the search should take us to the point of being able to reassemble all the separate pieces of ourselves. Wallace Fowlie defined the poet as one who was able to keep the fresh vision of the child alive within the mature man. I agree with that except during trauma, when pieces break off—so it's really a work of connectiveness.

EWJ: There is an almost archetypal cycle of return to the self at the inner core of your work.

AN: If our mythological journey is supposed to have been through the labyrinth we would ultimately come out, we would have to come out with all of ourselves, we couldn't leave parts of ourselves behind in the labyrinth.

EWJ: You mention in the diaries that you're a Pisces. Do you attribute any of the quality of flow and movement in your writing to the fact that you are a Pisces?

AN: I am very related to water. I feel very close to the sea, I like the idea of travelling and moving about, the whole journey on water. I think it has an influence on my wanting my writing to be fluid, not static. I felt that I wrote better on a houseboat because I could feel the river flowing underneath. I have been described as a Neptunian, for whom illusion was more important than the world of reality, and where the meshing of the dream and reality takes place.

EWJ: What is the source of your inexhaustible energy?

AN: I haven't thought about that. I guess it's curiosity, the fact that I still feel things as keenly. I suppose that when you feel alive something propels you into new experiences, new friendships, and while you're responding you have this energy. It seems to be a quality of responsiveness, of remaining alive to whatever is happening around you. While you have that feeling, you go on exploring. Then, I'm always curious. I was in an airplane accident once. There was only one wheel, one side of the wing had caught fire, we had six minutes to get to Los Angeles, and all I was doing was thinking of all the places I hadn't seen yet. That

Out of the Labyrinth: An Interview

was my feeling—that it was a shame not to see everything, to hear everything, be everywhere.

EWJ: What are you presently working on?

AN: I'm editing Volume Six [of *The Diary of Anaïs Nin*]. Editing Volume Seven will bring me to the exchange of letters and diaries with other women. Then I will go back and redo my childhood and adolescence, because readers say I started the diary at the point where my life expanded. They would like to see how it went from the narrow to the expanded part.

EWJ: How does it feel to have achieved recognition as a major literary figure?

AN: Well, I never imagined that. It's a lovely feeling, you lose your sense of isolation. And you can live out your universal life. You're in contact with the whole world, which is probably the wish of every writer. I have a feeling of being in touch with the world.

The Suicide Academy

We have had too many pedestrian novels in an age of space travel. Daniel Stern is able to toss all the facts into space, to reverse their chronological monotony, to upset established curricula. To consider the off-balance of the absurd as human, black humor as a daily contingency, terror and death from new positions, may reveal new techniques for defeating destruction. Daniel Stern's wit is not cold, or inhuman. He belongs to the new generation which is emotional, writing to be enjoyed, to surprise, to jolt, to charge and recharge. He uses mockery only to leap over the traps, not to separate us from experience.

The Suicide Academy is a place where would-be suicides are invited for a day of self-examination and meditation, after which they must decide whether to return to the world or to put an end to their lives. "Here you'll learn to live or die—and more—/You'll learn the truth: that one of them is best."

A group of variegated characters is assembled who will have an explosive effect upon each other: Wolf Walker, director, his ex-wife, Jewel, her present husband, Max Car-

A review of *The Suicide Academy*, by Daniel Stern, in *The Village Voice*, 10 October 1968.

dillo, Gilliat, the anti-semitic Negro, Barbara, the director's pregnant mistress, and a longer list of patients than the Academy was prepared to cope with. Appropriately, the landscape is all snow and ice.

The point of view is multilateral and reality is multidimensional. In this game of the intelligence played by our own illogic, when Wolf Walker wakes he establishes the stability of ambivalence:

He had been dreaming that Jewel was singing. The song was "Après un Rêve" by Fauré, and the particular passage his sleep had snagged on was the repetition of the word *reviens, reviens*. The note was middle C.

That was how I was going to begin this. But I don't think I can tell what happened at the Suicide Academy in that elegiac tone.

Here we slip into a surrealist world, relativity without center of gravity. We are dealing with the absurd, the irrelevant, the allegorical chaos of a world whose past hypocritical semblance of logic we can no longer accept. We are inside the Magic Theater of *Steppenwolf*, inside the nightmares of Kafka but in American equivalents—that is, with the weightlessness of humor. The psychological ironies are as accurate as they should be in a twentieth-century mind. The choice between life and death, creation and destruction, is always our own, but we prefer to blame other forces. *The Suicide Academy* invites us to meditate on the depth of our predicament, not in the seclusion of an old monastery but in an imaginary, transitional wayside station and in the center of drama, crisis, prejudices, distortions habitual to our daily life. It is not a meditation in quietness or isolation, although the snow landscape is vividly present and eloquent, as if its coolness were necessary to assuage the fevers and infections caught in active life. The place where we are

to make our decision is invaded by visitors whose aim remains a mystery. There is no haven of objectivity or abstract cerebrations. Absurdity pursues and surrounds them
all. The youthful, contemporary quality of the book lies in
its main objective, which is to enjoy, not to explain, to *be
with* all the happenings and to love whatever happens: Relationships which fail to catalyze, loves which miss their
targets, wrestling matches which establish no victor, talks
which add to distortions, ideologies which increase confusion, explanations which do not lead to a truce, all of them
are there as in daily life, but Daniel Stern gives them the
ebullience of wit, they float like lifesavers infused with the
oxygen of lyrical delight. The dead clichés by which people
defend themselves from change are bombarded in atomic
dissolutions to invent new dynamics. Turning ideas upside
down empties them of stale air and makes room for oxygen.
The desperate aspect of our destructive impulses is trans-
figured into an allegorical dance on the snow, a tribal dance
of desire. The message is directed to the senses: For example, we rediscover love through the strands of Jewel's hair.
Escapes, flights, evasions, the contemporary habit of splitting
experience into a happening and of filming the happening,
all is familiar. Max, the villain, is the film maker. "He shot
them in quick, nervous clicks, like a spy recording some
secret site on forbidden film. . . . [Were Max and Jewel]
innocent film-makers or guilty film-takers?
". . . camera madness, focusing, clicking, and winding."
The whole group is swept into a surrealist voyage. It is
not the walled-in nightmares of Kafka, constricted or claus-
trophobic. It is a dream of space, open, dazzling white land-
scapes, a mise-en-scène of joy, physical euphoria, muscular
energy, in sharp ironic contrast to the constant presence of
inarticulate and secret despairs.
Jewel is full of seduction, as she should be, and allergic

The Suicide Academy

85

to truth. "[Her] entire self was tangled up in her body. . . . She was the triumph of the apparent: utterly white skin, absolutely blue eyes, blonde hair that was the complete absence of black, of darkness." Jewel, allergic to truth as a man-made formula, not suited to her feminine labyrinth, her feminine need to be created.

The ballet Jewel and Wolf, her ex-husband, dance on the ice is a lyrical flight: ". . . we loped out onto the ice like a team of fugitive figure skaters who had forgotten how to describe the classic figures and so were inventing new ones. Was there a figure Z? I'm sure we created one. Or a figure R_2? I'm sure we invented it."

In every intelligent book, the key lies within. I am certain this is true of *The Suicide Academy*. It invents new figures. This is the secret of its elating effect. If during their marriage Wolf had refused to create Jewel as she had wished, now that she is contemplating suicide and has only one day in which to enact it or repudiate it, he is willing to create her at last and circumvent her own destruction. "I would operate, skillfully using memory, the arsenal of emotions, untapped hopes, buried hatreds masquerading in other guises, misplaced loves: the scalpels and sutures of my particular practice."

A key to the book, possibly its definition, can be found in these passages:

Suicide was a grand, dark continent to be charted and I was its cartographer.

Suicides were the aristocrats of death—God's graduate students, acting out their theses to prove how limited were the alternatives. He had allowed Himself and His creatures. Their act was, at its best, superb literary criticism. At its worst—well, perhaps it was this blonde loveliness [Jewel] not yet defined, and dying of its lack of definition. Giving away to dust the lovely outlines of those ever-so-slightly conical breasts, those long and tapering legs, that rounded cheek curving to indentation of shadowed eyes . . . all because of lack of shape. No! Suicide must be more than mere abortion. Part of my job *had* to be to save people for their proper deaths.

The novel leaps from metaphysics to pugilism, from literature to jealousy, from race prejudice to mythology, from mental acrobatics to physical exertion to sensual adventures, disguising wisdom under its agilities. The central juggler never misses. He is dexterous and alive to the dangers of seeking new ideas, new sensations, new expressions. He is a figure skater of language.

The circle, you see, is at the heart of all human anguish. The sundial and the clock prove that if there were no circles there would be no time. If there were no time there would be no death. Thus—no circles, no death. . . . Most of our guests come to us suffering from circle fatigue. Repetition, full revolution and more repetition. . . . Then imagine the joy of the straight line: forward movement, change. Even if the straight line leads straight down into the earth. Think of it! An end to circles!

In one sense the novel belongs with the theater of the absurd, but in another sense it goes beyond that: The contemplation of man's irrationalities has another purpose. It is an exercise in imaginative freedom. Since logic has been proved by events to be another form of hypocrisy, this turning of ideas upside down to shake out falsities does not end up in negations but in potential liberations. It demonstrates that the habit of skillful questioning, juxtaposing, juggling is not a pastime but a serious need for the seeker of truth. The academy symbolically burns to the ground. Built on ambivalences, all that remains of it is what each man rescues for himself out of the ashes, a world in harmony with his emotional vision, meaningful to him alone so that he can juggle himself into balance. A surrealist world in fact, obvious in history, politics, economics, science, which the Director of the Argentine Academy sums up thus:

We must suspect that there is no universe in the organic, unifying sense inherent in that ambitious word. If there is, we must conjecture its purpose; we must conjecture the words, the definitions, the etymologies, the synonymies of God's secret dictionary . . .

In my cold fever, whether due to the heightening of my fears or to alcohol, I saw the landscape as a calligraphic wonder. The thinning line of trees casting elongated shadows on the snow, like a prayer book in a foreign language, but which one knew by legend to hold a famous and beautiful verse; the long line of uneven rocks scattered in a shaky hand, stretching from grass's end to the shore. First larger then smaller, light-burnished colors then blackened gleaming shades all straggled with seaweed, strophe and anti-strophe, unfinished statement of stone and sand. And the flights of sandpipers hurled at the sibilance of shore-froth hissing them back then enticing them to return to the edge, fragments of alien texts, sacred letters whose meaning had been forgotten, old feathered prophecies, creations of inspired astrologists of earlier generations. . . .

I told her, then, of my reading the landscape the way I read the sky when I was a child. Stuck with *logos* from the start, that was me. The world as untranslatable language.

We live in the midst of a black plague, a plague of hatred. This book is an antidote to the epidemic affecting us. Surrealism as a cure for nausea. *The Suicide Academy* is ultimately the book of a poet, which means he flies at an altitude above the storms of destruction, above neutrality, above indifference, and therefore beyond death.

Miss MacIntosh, My Darling

When a writer decides to give us a complete universe, all that he has explored and discovered, it is necessarily vast. No one ever questions the expanse of the ocean, or the size of a mountain. The key to the enjoyment of this amazing book is to abandon one's self to the detours, wanderings, elliptical and tangential journeys, accepting in return miraculous surprises. This is a search for reality through a maze of illusions and fantasy and dreams, ultimately asserting in the words of Calderon: "Life is a dream."

The necessity for the cellular expansion of the book lies in Marguerite Young's own words: "I just tried to leave pebbles along the road so that no one could get lost." For the perilous exploration of illusion and reality, the author's feeling is that if one is to follow the full swelling of the wave of imagination, one must bring back to the shore the wave which carried him. It is in the fullness and completeness of the motion that one achieves understanding.

That is why she is able to sustain, all through, both the rich deep tone and powerful rhythm of the book. This is a feat of patience, accomplished by weaving each connecting cell, with unbroken bridges, from word to word, image to

A review of *Miss MacIntosh, My Darling*, by Marguerite Young, in *Open City*, Los Angeles, 1 May 1968.

image, phrase to phrase. She is an acrobat of space and symbol but she gives her readers a safety net.

Although she accomplishes for native American folklore the same immortality of the myth that Joyce accomplished for Ireland's, Joyce was not her inspiration. Her inspiration was America, her middlewestern, down-to-earth America with its powerful orbital dreamers so rarely portrayed, born on native soil, American as Joyce's characters are Irish, with the American sense of high comedy, extravagance and vividness: the bus driver, the suffragette, the old maid, the composer of unwritten music, the clam digger, the dead gambler, the waitress, the featherweight champion, the hangman, the detective, the stone breaker, the messenger pigeon, the frog, the moose.

The work has a disappearing shore line. It is a submarine world, geographically situated in the unconscious and in the night. "The sea is not harmful if you sleep under it, not over it, best place for keeping pearls," says one of her characters.

The numerous characters enter one's own stream of consciousness and cannot be erased because they are part of the American psyche, a psyche, as Marguerite Young says, capable of the wildest fantasy. They are listed only in the Blue Book of the Uncommon. Marguerite Young is an aristocrat among writers, perhaps the precursor of a new era in American literature.

The book is also a canto to obsession. Life is filled with repetitions culminating in variations which indicate the subtlety of man's reactions to experience.

The characters are tangible, accessible, familiar. But it is the nature of their experience which Marguerite Young questions, its sediments, its echoes and reflections. What is reality? Deep within us it is as elusive as a dream, and we are not sure of anything that happened.

Angel in
the Forest

For those who had the unique experience of reading Marguerite Young's *Miss MacIntosh, My Darling,* her *Angel in the Forest,* published twenty years earlier, will be a prelude to the vaster work concerned with the exploration of reality and illusion. In *Miss MacIntosh, My Darling,* illusion stems from the opium dreams of the mother which had to be disentangled before the narrator could reach the end and purpose of her quest. This is a work of fiction. *Angel in the Forest* is a work of history. It deals with the creation of Utopia, which was America's first illusion. This is the story of Father Rapp and Robert Owen's two experiments in social science carried out in Indiana in the nineteenth century. The application of this theme to present-day problems makes it seem contemporary. When a poet chooses to write history, facts gain in power and in dimensions. Marguerite Young is a meticulous scholar, but she illumines every description and every character with the laser light of significance. Her facts radiate wit and irony and are incarnated in human beings.

A review of *Angel in the Forest,* by Marguerite Young, in the *Los Angeles Times,* 8 May 1966.

"Question—what is the nature of experience—what dream among dreams is reality?"

The place, New Harmony, is resurrected as if it had never faded. The title refers to giant footprints, said to have been those of an angel, on a stone which a humble stonecutter saved from total obliteration (or perhaps carved upon the stone himself?). Indiana is Marguerite Young's native land. With a few vivid lines she can summon up hundreds of its inhabitants, with their human foibles, idiosyncrasies, fallibilities, to show how they sabotage their own idealistic conceptions.

Mr. Pears, the bookkeeper dismissed for an error: "True he had drunk a little on the side now and then, but not enough to cause the dancing of arithmetic." Mrs. Pears, who thought "nothing so bad as despotism which pretends to be democracy." Together they show "a gradual waning of their hope for improvement at New Harmony." Human beings' own individual fantasies, hungers, obsessions, habits, defeat their own illusions. "Who, finally, was happy in New Harmony, a scene of conflict between individual and still-born collectivism?"

When the book was first printed, during a paper shortage, too few people were privileged to read it. It contains the seeds of the major work to which Marguerite Young gave the next seventeen years. History, she proved, is an aggregate of fictions, and she was to enter totally into the world of fiction where she found many of the sources of mysterious failures.

"William Taylor, in view of his belief in the relativism and subjectivism of happiness, and his distrust of any value but pleasure, proposed that the Owenites gathered around him should hold a funeral for the science of society, all merry drunks to be the mourners. *To build a coffin for the idea of all mankind, a featureless body, they worked as never before in the whole history of Utopia."*

The relation of this experiment to the present shows its timelessness. It was necessary to bring out of the oceanic depths of the subconscious the sorcerer's apprentices who undermined all social experiments. The author's two books invite us to sit at a giant conference table and parley with them. This conference table is also a banquet table, serving in crystalline style characters whose footprints to our own door Marguerite Young has carved.

Edgar Varèse

To recognize the unique value of a man and an artist, most people wait for the perspective of distance and time. But those friends of Edgar Varèse who were aware of how strikingly the personality of the man and his music matched each other, had a more immediate clue to his true stature and unique place in the history of music. He was a man who lived in a vast universe, and because of the height of his antennae he could encompass past, present, and future. I could feel this each time I rang the bell of his home and he opened the door, for if he received me with the warmth he showed to all his friends, at the same time I could hear all around him and flowing out of the house an ocean of sound not created for one person, one room, one house, one street, one city, or one country, but for the cosmos. His large, vivid, blue-green eyes flashed not only with the pleasure of recognition but with a signal welcoming me into a universe of new vibrations, new tones, new effects, new ranges, in which he himself was completely immersed. He led me into his workroom. The piano took most of the space, and on the music stand there was always a piece of

From *Perspectives of New Music*, Princeton University Press, Spring–Summer 1966.

musical notations. They were in a state of revision resembling a collage: all fragments, which he had arranged and rearranged and displaced until they achieved a towering construction. I always looked with delight at these fragments, which were also tacked on the board above his worktable and on the walls, because they expressed the very essence of his work and character: they were in a state of flux, mobility, flexibility, always ready to fly into a new metamorphosis, free, obeying no monotonous sequence or order except his own. The tape recorder would be on high volume for open spaces. He wanted one possessed by, absorbed into, its oceanic waves and rhythms. Edgar Varèse would demonstrate a new bell, a new object capable of giving forth a new tonality, new nuance. He was in love with his materials, with an indefatigable curiosity. In his workroom one became another instrument, a container, enclosed in his orbital flights into sound.

When we climbed the small stairway to the living room and dining room to join other friends, greeted by his gentle and gracious wife, Louise, Varèse the composer became Varèse the conversationalist. He radiated in company, he was eloquent, satirical, and witty. There was a harmony between his work and his talk. He had contempt only for clichés in music or in thought. His revolt against the cliché never ceased. He used vivid, pungent language. He retained the revolutionary boldness of youth, but always directed by his intelligence and discrimination, never blind or inaccurate. He never destroyed anything but mediocrity, hypocrisy, and false values. He attacked only what deserved to be attacked, and never in personal, petty or blind anger, as is practiced by some artists today.

Speaking once of an unsavory political character he said, "A faire vomir une boîte a ordure."

His wars were on a high level; they were waged against

the men who always stood in the way of vast original projects because they could neither perceive them nor control them.

The last talk we had together was about the irony of the foundations and universities not giving him a complete electronic workshop to work with. He was filled with concepts he could not carry out for lack of the necessary facilities. He needed the machines which were so easily entrusted to young, unformed musicians. He needed a laboratory for exploration into future sounds. Most of these young men could not feed the machines, only run them, and Varèse could have fed them with endless volcanic richness.

Many musical experts will write about what Varèse composed. I would like to stress what he was not allowed to create, because every artist dreams of being emptied of all his riches before he dies, and when he leaves us, carrying into oblivion untapped treasures, it should arouse our sense of guilt. Varèse knew the blindness which besets most people in the presence of creative giants. I told him the story of a dinner I had attended for members of a famous corporation set up to produce new inventions. After moulding their men to standard forms, disciplining them, inhibiting them, they were trying to find a way to get spontaneous, creative ideas out of them. The men, reduced to automatons, sat at a conference table and someone shouted at them, "Don't think, say the first thing which comes to your mind, anything," and this grotesque effort even had a technical name. Naturally, nothing could come from men who had long ago lost their power to create. I suggested they call in the artists I knew who were overfull of ideas, designs, etc. There was a silence. "Oh, yes, we know," they said, "you mean those mad geniuses who will not wear a clean shirt and a tie, will not come in on time and *cannot be controlled*." "Controlled" was the revealing word. In music too, everyone turned to the men who could be controlled—disciples, imitators, derivatives. They never dared to consult the source from which creation and invention issued like some great phenomenon of nature, the highest waterfalls, the highest mountains, the deepest canyons, the bottomless lakes. Every artist has known this isolation in which giants are left as if they were dangerous creatures. A more familiar, homelier connection could be made with the innocuous, and the hack printer was easier to deal with than the original painter. It would have required a critic, a listener, a conductor, or a foundation director of equal stature to approach the artist who is, by natural rights of the creator, the dictator in his own province. How frightened we are of a revolutionary force in full eruption.

Varèse was merciless towards the timid, the flabby, and the impotent. He would say: "They have handed the whole business to mechanics. The new machines need composers who can nourish them." This was the substance of our last talk. It was the first time I noticed that at eighty-one he stooped, but it was from illness. He was wise enough to know men's fears. He knew they would approach him when they were no longer in danger of being swept into the resonant coils of his sound flights. He is now an archetype, whose potentials were not exploited by the world, but what he left belongs to the same vast cosmology which science is seeking to charter. For every new discovery we need new sounds, and Varèse heard them before the undiscovered spaces were reached. He said gently once: "There is no avant garde. There are only people who are a little late."

Light travels faster than sound, but in the case of Varèse, sound travelled much faster.

At a Journal Workshop

After contributing several valuable books on psychology and teaching depth psychology at Drew University, Ira Progoff has evolved a remarkable method using the intensive journal to unify the personality and effectively achieve a kind of self-therapy.

He begins by eliminating the idea of the journal as a literary achievement, so that anyone from any walk of life and with any degree of education can complete a "mirror image" of his life and character, make a synthesis of experiences and dreams, and arrive at a self-creation, which until now were seriously hampered by the absurd puritan taboo against self-development and the pursuit of the inner journey—supposedly expressions of narcissism or neurotic subjectivity. This book, the result of years of experience with the expansion and development of journal writing, proves that an inner journey into the labyrinth of the self can mean maturity, the understanding of experience, the cohesive action of a reporting, an examination, a confrontation of one's experience. The erroneous concept that extroverted

A review of *At a Journal Workshop: The Basic Text and Guide for Using the Intensive Journal,* by Ira Progoff, in the *Los Angeles Times,* 19 October 1975.

life is superior to the exploration, and therefore creation, of the self was disproved by the disintegration of the personality which dominates our culture, dependency on therapy, confusion, and chaos. Progoff's method is highly spiritual in its concept. It is in effect far more selfless than the artificial objectivity of those who believe that by not writing about themselves they contribute more to society than by creating a harmonious self.

From the very beginning, *At a Journal Workshop* establishes the motive for the inner journey; the first chapter is titled "The Intensive Journal as an Instrument for Life." What follows is a series of suggestions for ways to record our experiences, our memories, our dreams, as keys to an understanding of our lives. Progoff has illuminating suggestions such as: "Loosening the Soil of our Life," "Listing the Steppingstones," "The Life History Log," "Intersections: Roads Taken and not Taken," "Reconstructing our Autobiography." His book achieves a therapeutic effect "not by striving towards therapy but by providing active techniques that enable an individual to draw upon his inherent resources for becoming a whole person." No one, in this era of chaos and confusion, will question the value of bringing a whole person to the collective life.

"Many persons have already had experiences in which they sensed the presence of an underlying reality in life, a reality which they have recognized as a personal source of meaning and strength."

"The Intensive Journal is specifically designed to provide an instrument and techniques by which persons can discover within themselves the resources they did not know they possessed." Again Progoff reminds us that "the essence lies not in the events of his life in themselves, not in the things that ever happened to him, but in his inner relationship to those events."

At a Journal Workshop

The atmosphere he tries to create during weekend seminars is that of a group, a group which does not spend its time in talk but in writing journals, in meditating. The companionship is there, but it is not dissipated in talk.

There is an intelligent self-creation behind the Intensive Journal, one usually achieved by long drawn-out therapy, "the experience of drawing the present situation of your life into focus."

One cannot help being amazed by what emerges from this skillful inner journey. All the elements we attribute to the poet, the artist, become available to everyone, to all levels of society.

The level and quality of each individual life is revealed by Progoff. Consulting with dreams, dialogues with lost parents or figures of wisdom, meditating, and the beautiful exploration of what he calls "Twilight Imagery," all give each life a poetry, a beauty, a spiritual content which has been totally lacking in our culture because of suspicion of subjectivity. One can see so clearly the life being created, becoming a beautiful, cohesive story. To explore its meaning heightens all experience. Lack of self-confidence or self-respect vanishes.

The Journal Workshop becomes a sanctuary, "for it provides a protected situation safe from the pressures of the world in which an individual can quietly reappraise his relation to his life."

To witness the rich material, the images, the dreams which are called forth in this situation from individuals who never knew they possessed such inward riches, is to put to shame those who worked so persistently at destroying all inner life in favor of activity and blind extroversion, creating a culture prey to brain washing of the lowest quality by the media, a people who could not think or judge for themselves and who became the blind followers of corrupt forces.

"The Tao of Growth." The self begins to appear like a fruit or a plant, but unlike these, the human being experiences obstacles, traumatic events which arrest his growth. The Intensive Journal encourages a rhythm, a continuity, which in turn becomes a natural flow. In recording experiences, one is urged forward, urged to move. "Physical growth is easy to recognize, but personal growth is inward and elusive."

One of the most impressive results of Ira Progoff's method is that every life acquires a value, a richness. The "Twilight Imagery" encourages the imagination, the visualization, which lies beyond our consciousness. The greatest lack in our culture is the sense of meaningfulness, which leads to hopelessness and indifference, often to more serious criminality. The miracle of understanding and cohesion, of centering the self, is the pride it acquires, its renewed sense of dignity and of the potential of human beings. "Outward activity propelled from within is the essence of a creative existence."

Progressing from "Dream Log," "Twilight Imagery Log," "Imagery Extensions," and "Inner Wisdom Dialogue," the self unfolds like a surprising cache of treasures long buried and unused.

One of Progoff's most striking symbols is the well. We go into our individual wells as deeply as we can, and instead of finding ourselves cut off from the world we reach the universal waters which feed wells. "It is the image of the well connecting to the underground stream."

The other miracle is that as we intensify our understanding and creation of the self, we understand and communicate with others with far more intuition and wisdom. "We each must go through our own personal existence, but when we have gone deeply enough we find that we have gone through our personal life beyond our personal life." The construction of a cohesive self becomes a source of strength to meet destructive or tragic experiences or losses. "The key to Twilight Imagery lies in the fact that it takes place in the twilight state between waking and sleeping. We find that by working actively in that intermediate state of consciousness, we are able to reach depths in ourselves, depths which are very difficult to contact by any other means."

The fascination of this method lies in the discovery of a self we did not know lay within us. It is an adventure into unexplored, undiscovered spheres. It becomes a source of strength, courage, and pride. "As much as possible, our writing should focus on the essence of the experience." One of the obstacles to this inner journey has been people's lack of confidence in their writing ability. But Progoff has foreseen this and reminds us that "the daily log is not an exercise in literature; it is an exercise in our lives."

No one has analyzed the fascination of fiction; and no one, until Progoff developed this structure, has realized that our lives can become as interesting as any biography or fiction we read with such interest. It is a matter of seeing one's life as a metaphor, as a tale, as a story of enormous drama. This is in relation to the meaningfulness of any life which is examined and recorded with care. The other benefic aspect is that the cumulative effect "is to draw our life into focus so that we have a basis for making the decisions that are pressing at the moment."

One of the most inspiring chapters deals with the steppingstones of our life. "The steppingstones are the significant points of movement along the road of an individual's life."

Progoff emphasizes the need to eliminate all censorship and judgments. He believes these are inhibiting factors, overused by a narrow-minded culture and harmful to the spontaneous creation of the self. He stresses this throughout the book. There is a difference between judgment and evaluation; evaluation is creative, judgment is not.

Another inspiring sequence is "Intersections: Roads Taken and not Taken" which opens rich sources of meditation. "We go back over the road of our life looking for unlived possibilities." The study of these movements is invaluable because, as Progoff says, "it is not always easy to recognize the intersections in our lives because we are often not aware of their being intersections at the time they occur."

The physical atmosphere surrounding the work is also important. Progoff stresses first of all relaxation, then closed eyes, and finally the silence and quiet necessary to the inward journey.

Following his pattern recreates all that our memory, our consciousness, have discarded, revealing a treasure chest of dreams, thoughts, memories, experiences. In denying the need of intimacy with ourselves, our extroverted culture destroys the possibility of intimacy with others. This valuable experiment, which recreates a human being, inevitably enables one human being to perceive more in others' lives.

The overuse of therapy came from our inability to put order and cohesion in our own lives, from an inability to develop an intimate knowledge of ourselves, from having no place to commune with our unmasked selves. This communion is vitally essential. Progoff guides us along the way of this spiritual discipline.

Having learned to commune with ourselves, we step into a wide range of dialogues: Some dialogues might complete dialogues which were interrupted by a death or a quarrel or whatever; others might be with any person of our choice. "We carry around within ourselves the traces of relationships that have unfulfilled potentialities." We learn of an infinite number of dialogues, with some lost by death, with others lost by estrangement, with figures of wisdom, with those who influenced our lives.

The lack of intimacy with one's self and consequently with others is what created the loneliest and most alienated people in the world. Progoff ultimately proves that "the process of growth in a human being, the process out of which a person emerges, is essentially an inward process."

With this book anyone can learn to extract meaning from his life. "Now let us sit in silence. Our eyes are closed. Our breathing slower and slower. In the quietness our attention is drawn inward."

And where does this lead? To the transpersonal meaning of our existence. "We have moved from the purely personal to the deeper than personal level of our experience." We know that our generation has been preoccupied with "how we can gain access to the potentials of knowledge contained in the depth of us, how we can achieve increased capacities of direct intuition and enlarged awareness."

When, after the publication of my diaries, I was asked to lecture, the one question I could never answer is illumined by this book: How? How to begin, how to expand, how to develop journal writing?

Henry Jaglom: Magician of the Film

From the early beginnings of the motion picture film, Antonin Artaud said that only films would be able to depict dreams, fantasies, the surrealist aspect of our experience. But very soon they veered away from that magic power and turned to one-dimensional stories. Very few made attempts to penetrate the deeper layers of our way of experiencing life. Yet it was the perfect medium for capturing our inner life. We know, we are aware of how our lives are an intermingling of dream, reality, illusion, fantasy, childhood influences, and wishes. As soon as I saw *A Safe Place*, I knew this was the film which attempted to penetrate that level and did so with unusual sensitivity and skill. It was a perfect fusion. It was the perfect superimposition of memory, dream, illusion, and the grappling with reality.

The writer-director Henry Jaglom accomplishes the extraordinary feat while situating his story in the most ordinary of all backgrounds: Central Park, New York, and the roofs of apartment houses in New York. This magic transformation of reality by the dream, he tells us, can take place anywhere. It is in Central Park that the magician, who so

A review of *A Safe Place*, written and directed by Henry Jaglom, in the *Los Angeles Free Press*, 6 October 1972.

deeply affects the child in the woman, Noah, practices his skills. There is a delightful humor in the magician's relation to the zoo animals. There are tender and wistful scenes, as when the girl shows her secret box in which she keeps her wish and the young man wants to open it. She knows that the day it is opened it might be empty, as the magician's hands are occasionally empty. There is a beautiful scene in which she hides in a closet from the luxury and art of the young man's background, which does not reach her, and where she contemplates the nature of love as it is expressed in different eyes. The writing here is that of a poet.

The theme, which runs through the film like a musical motif and gives the many-leveled story its continuity, is the constant return to the magician, to the real bond between the girl and the magician because he can make a ball fly in the air. Noah bounces back from every encounter with love to the magician who performed for her when she was a child. She is obsessed with the memory that as a child she was able to fly in a tree from one branch to another. She insists the rational young man who loves her should believe this. It is important that he believe this. The symbolism of what she is trying to reach, to assert, to seek, is deeply moving: She seeks a dimension in life in which dream and reality are fused. He cannot follow her. There is a scene in which they both improvise on telephone prefixes and he flunks the poetry test. Everything in the film has to be interpreted as we interpret dreams.

One of the great seductions of the film is the perfection of atmosphere and poetic elements. The simplicity of the realistic scenes, a table at an open-air restaurant, a sun deck, and their facile replacement by a scene of fantasy. The hunger for magic. Noah's recognition that she cannot love in a human way: No one has found the key to the locked box which she is for others. There is in the film great mobility, fluidity, a sensuous dwelling on color, light, facial expressions, with an original use of silence. The accompaniment of music and the flow of the images serve to connect these worlds which we have kept separate.

In most films, what takes place in our feelings, the imagery of our dreams around events, is rarely filmed. We know it is an external image, we know the dimensions are missing, that it is hard as a wall. We are not stirred deeply. The depths have been left untouched. Here it is this depth which is touched, it affects one almost subconsciously, it is the dream which is captured. We become aware of what we aspire to, seek, may or may not find.

The magician's only failure is that he cannot make things disappear. In the world of childhood wishes they visit the zoo together, the most humorous part of the film. The elephant, the lion, and the llama do not disappear. He does make one lover disappear, but this is the lover who disappears anyway after each encounter.

But the wish to disappear has been transferred to the girl. When she meets with love divided, the lover who does not love, and the lover whom she cannot love in return, she thinks of disappearing. The realistic lover who asserted flying was an impossibility, at the end, like Sancho Panza with Don Quixote, from association with her, begins to believe that she could fly. That she disappears in death seems natural. Magic has failed her, but at least she can disappear.

The actors give extraordinary performances. They suggest their characters immediately and in depth. They are deprived of the artificial continuity and explanations—literal chronological and passport identifications—relished by other films. It is an impressionistic film. An X ray of our psychic life, which gives an insight instantly into the secret self.

Henry Jaglom: Magician of the Film

Those who may be irritated are those who have always feared the depths and who, in spite of so many proofs to the contrary, think we live in a rational world. Better to face the minotaur of our dreams and know their fragility and gain a deeper understanding of the human dilemma.

What makes for loneliness, this film says, is our inability to share our dreams. Those who fail to understand this film will drive themselves and others to the safe place of non-existence.

Un Chant d'Amour

Jean Genêt's film *Un Chant d'Amour* proves that true morality lies in aesthetics, not in the nature of the experience. The beauty and power of this film of homosexual love captures the very essence of love through its sincerity and absence of vulgarity. Genêt is a poet of the erotic and has created a canto to love with so much pride and style that it expresses ultimately the beauty of all desire. The only morality is that of the great artist who can-arouse pride in sensual expression. He never offends the senses as many other films have done by their repellent weakness or humiliating ugliness. Genêt's film is a film of virility. That is the important theme. The prisoners could be any men— and the prison the cells which society erects between men to the detriment of their love. The men in prison are vital, filled with love; and ironically the guard is the only perverted figure: he does not love or desire, he is the voyeur— jealous, envious, impotent. He can only punish what he does not possess. This is the most unrestrained film I have ever seen, but Genêt's vigor, naturalness, and great sense of beauty give it a ritualistic, classical nobility. It converts ex-

A review of *Un Chant d'Amour*, written and directed by Jean Genêt, in the *Los Angeles Free Press*, 24 December 1965.

perience into a symbolic action. By the choice of men of quality, vitality, intensity, he is saying we imprison what is alive because it is dangerous to those who are not.

There is poetry and sensitiveness in the exchange of symbolic acts: pushing a straw through the prison wall, breathing the smoke of a cigarette as a carrier of the breath of desire, swinging flowers from window to window just beyond the reach of thirsty hands. What casts a shadow of ugliness in other films results from the attitude and vision of the film maker. Puritanism paints in ugly colors. Here the Negro's priapic dance in his cell untainted by hypocrisy assumes the stature of a pagan ritual. The contrast between the destructive, sadistic impulses of the guard and the primitive, lyrical outbursts of the prisoners indicates that fine shading between impotence and virility, life and disease. When stated by a poet who accepts the full expression of desire as an act of life, it becomes as naked as nature—and as innocent. If all experience could pass through the censorship of art, it would achieve what the law has been unable to do. It would assert the need of beauty. It would teach that the only vice is ugliness, and it would automatically rid us of the caricatures of sex which have been passing for eroticism and restore to sensuality its nobility, which lies in the quality and refinement of its expression, the refinement of wholeness.

The cells become a tragic enclosure, separating man from life, from joy. At the film's most sadistic moment, a prisoner being whipped by a guard dreams of woodlands, sunlight, and pagan fulfillment. It is the guard who, unable to attain this, can only wield a gun as a symbol of virility, can only destroy because he is incapable of desire.

Ingmar Bergman

The greater part of the world lives pretending to be guided by reason. The artist has always been telling us that we live by nonrational impulses.

We are more apt to believe it when a man like Senator Fulbright makes this statement: "I know by what means we can stop war but I also know that human beings live by irrational impulses." The greatest need we have is to examine this irrational source of our acts with the hope that by confronting them we will be able to understand and wield an intelligent control over them. But while we continue to ignore and suppress them, they will wreck our lives. Bergman is one of the most fearless adventurers into the realm of the irrational, to the extremes of passionate experience.

Our culture has a particular distaste for tragedy and extremes of emotion, it avoids exploring the unconscious, will not portray actions not analyzable by the intellect. But as D. H. Lawrence said, passionate experience must come first, and analysis afterwards. What Bergman gives us is an entry into the very heart and core of passionate experience.

A lecture given at the UCLA Hommage to Bergman, 12 October 1973.

The critics are annoyed by mystery. If significance eludes them they feel powerless, but mystery is the proof of man's spiritual existence and symbolism is the only way to capture it, and the language must be learned. But one must first of all accept immersion into the night world of the unconscious. You cannot analyze while feeling. John Simon, who has best understood Bergman, says in his book, *Ingmar Bergman Directs:* "The superficial, popular notion of Bergman, sparked perhaps by such irresponsible criticism, is as a maker of misty, symbolic, pretentious inscrutabilities . . ."

This is because we demand answers *before* we enter into the labyrinth of the interior journey, we demand sign posts and street signs. Bergman's films, as Simon says, are open-ended films abutting on unanswerable questions. Who has answered such questions as: Is there a god? Is there an afterlife? If the solution to our problems is love, what kind of love, and how can it be achieved? If we find peace in work, artistic creation, closeness to nature, the circle of friends or the family circle, just how do we go about accomplishing this?

Bergman is saying that we are intelligent enough to pursue our own examination of the experience he makes us undergo. He asks you to *suffer* it, because he knows that if you do not enter experience with emotion, but only with the mind, it will not change you. He communicates directly with your unconscious. The one who seeks only analytical clarity remains a tourist, a spectator. I assume from the misunderstanding of Bergman that many are more comfortable as tourists and do not wish to stir, awaken, disturb, the obscure selves we do not even acknowledge within ourselves.

Another thing which is foreign to us (obsessed with collective mass history) is Bergman's interest in what Simon calls the "chamber film, derived from chamber music, which means an intense focus upon one, two, or four persons, the action confined in time and space and the story intensely intimate."

Once we become aware of the enormous importance of music for Bergman, we can better understand that he intends that we should receive his films as we receive music. It should reach us directly as music does, touching the centers of emotion, bypassing analytic dissection by the mind. We have to tune in to Bergman differently than we tune in to one-dimensional films.

By affecting us as music does, he brings us into intimate contact with a few people. In *Cries and Whispers* we become intimate as never before with the process of dying. We become intimate with the meaning of compassion, expressed by the servant, which not even religion has been able to convey with such human power. No saint has given the depth of human love given by the servant. Bergman wants you to feel with him and to dream with him. He will not tell you when the dream begins or ends. For him life, dream, and art are identical. Whether consciously or unconsciously, we live by an intermingling of them, what the surrealist calls "superimpositions."

He refuses to establish boundaries. He feels that dream and action are interrelated, fantasy and madness, creation and destruction. As his role is to make our subconscious life visible, as visible as the conscious, he does not paint it as a ghostly presence. When he dresses the four sisters in white against a red background it is not only a realistic description of the dress and background of their epoch, it expresses the idea that although apparently related, they are total strangers to each other. The unity of a family is an illusion. The dying sister's dream was that they should merge as sisters; that they should commune and by emotional unity defeat the disintegration of death. Her dream was not to be fulfilled, but we receive a subliminal message: Love and communion alone could have defeated the annihilation of death. When two of the sisters seem to break the barrier, talk and weep together, and appear to have achieved intimacy, then one of them, upon leaving, closes the door completely upon this intimacy and destroys it by mockery.

The mystery is there and Bergman asks us to contemplate it. If we contemplate mystery long enough our own creativity will set about unravelling it. Part of the mystery is that he takes us into the act of birth, birth of a film as well as of a character. In *Persona* he begins with a mystifying set of images like the quick recall of our life we are supposed to have before death. He is taking you into the mind of the film maker, remembering, meditating, into the fumbling process of the birth of a film, because the theme will emerge as a study of art and life, of the conflict between illusion and reality.

I am not here to analyze or unravel the characters Bergman portrays. I am here to ask you to receive them as he intended you to receive them. He has described them as his dreams. He honors your intelligence by leaving the interpretation to you.

He has chosen to place mostly upon women the burden of experience: pregnancy, rape, hysteria, psychic insight, alienation, non-love, passion, frustration. Women easily identify with Bergman's women. He has painted all of them. Was he aware that Freud (the unjustly maligned) said women had remained in closer contact with their unconscious than men? They recognize their obsessions, their fantasies, their sexual frustrations, their ambivalences, their sacrifices, their masochism.

He respects the shadows. He makes us the gift of intense experiences others will not touch, such as the theme of humiliation human beings practice upon each other, the theme of repression, of hidden cruelties, of dualities.

The great beauty of Bergman's films is that he goes to the very end of emotional experience. He touches bottom.

He treats nothing lightly, not even sensual dalliance. Compare *Smiles of a Summer Night* with Max Ophul's *La Ronde*. With all its charm and rhythm *La Ronde* is like a ride on a merry-go-round.

John Simon tells us that Bergman was reading Jung at the time he composed *Persona*. He may have been inspired to study the roles human beings play for the benefit of others as well as to satisfy the expectations of his own conscious self.

Many times Bergman has described the infinitely subtle interchange, the merging and submerging of one personality into another, projections and identifications. In *Persona* he focussed on this exchange of souls and confusion of identities. He delves deeply into the theme of withdrawal and failed interchange. He does not tell us if the women exchanged souls, whether the actress recovered her capacity to feel or talk, whether the nurse learned you cannot rescue others by love. Bergman does not reach for the ultimate answers. He enters the labyrinth, he exposes the mysterious influences, the deep layers of secret angers and doubts, the hungers, fears, needs. We are given a physical expression of an elusive psychic drama. For the first time we become aware of the murderous intent of silence, the exigencies of love's demands.

In what other films have we dealt with what Simon describes as the conflict between acting and being, art and life, illusion and reality, between sickness and health, lies and truths, concealing and revealing, between being and nonbeing, creation and destruction, life and death?

One of the most important aims of psychoanalysis is not an intellectual process; it urges us to relive suppressed experiences, to re-enact emotionally what we had failed to feel. It is the emotional, not the analytical, journey which brings deliverance from secret corrosions. Bergman's films have that intent; we should accept the fact of a profound emotional journey into mostly unexplored realms, into all we have not dared to feel, to say, to act, to embrace in life. It is a journey through dark regions. But it should stir in us all the unknown elements in ourselves. So few of us go to the very extremes of love, obsession, cruelty, alienation, jealousy, self-destruction. The psychic, unconscious world made visible is bound to startle us as this is the world which Jung has called our shadow. Bergman presents the shadow of the selves we do not wish to acknowledge. Let us at least allow them to live in his films, and recognize how richly they have affected and changed us. For whoever makes our dreams visible and audible illuminates and helps to make us master of our own unconscious life.

Enchanted
Places

The Labyrinthine City of Fez

Fez was created for the delight of our five senses. My first impression is a fragrant odor of cedarwood from the furniture of the Hotel Palais Jamai, a smell that reappears in the *souk*, or street, amidst the intense activity of the carpenters. My room already bears the colors of Fez: blue tile, copper tray, copper-colored draperies. When I open them, the whole city of Fez lies before my eyes. The earth-colored houses huddle together, following the sinuosities of the hills, encircling every now and then a mosque with its minaret of green tiles shining in the setting sun. On the terraces are draped what I mistook for trailing bougainvillea and which turned out to be dyed skins and wools drying in the sun, draped over the walls and ramparts of the city like bright cherry vines.

The minarets are numerous, three hundred or so, one for each quarter, giving the sense of protection and serenity so characteristic of the Islamic religion. Fez lies very still. It is a city of silence, which makes it appear more and more like an illustration from the Bible. The draped figures in their varicolored jellabas keep their age and weight a secret. They could be sketched by a child who has never learned

From *Travel & Leisure*, October/November 1973.

drawing: a blotch of color against the landscape, moved by the wind, women's faces hidden in *ltem*, or veils, the men's faces hidden by burnouses. It is a life bent towards inner self-perfection, whose dynamic activity lies in the skill, the incredible creative activity of their hands.

The hotel is high above Fez because it was once the palace of the vizier, and he could see the entire city from his terrace. A new hotel has been added right next to the old, but the ancient one can be visited. It has a room with encrustations of gold in the ceiling; and the favorite's room in the garden, with its deep rose and red rugs like a carpet of flowers from Persian fairy tales, its dark, sumptuous bed with a shell-like headpiece encrusted with copper and mother-of-pearl, exhaling the perfume of cedarwood, its copper myriad-eyed lamps diffusing a soft jewelled light, the many pillows of damask and silk, the low divans, the ornamentation enriched by the lovingly carved wood, by stucco, and by meticulous tile work. There is a cabinet of cedarwood, deep and ample, for the favorite's jewels.

Because the souks of Fez are a maze, it is necessary to have a guide. Only those born in this ancient city can find their way. The streets were built narrow originally for coolness against the relentless sun. Some of the ninth-century streets are only a yard and a half wide. As soon as you step out of the hotel courtyard, with a handsome, tall guide dressed in a brown wool jellaba and bright canary yellow *babouches*, or slippers, you enter the *medina*, or old Arab city. The beauty of this labyrinth is that it takes you into a world of crafts and arts and awakens your five senses every bit of the way. Every small boutique, sometimes as small as eight feet by eight, is a revelation of some skill. Men are sewing the embroidered caftans worn by the women, with gold braids, embroidered edges, trimmings of colored sequins. The transparent chiffon and gauze dresses worn by the dancers are made to shine like jewels, and as they hang in front of the boutiques they seem like pennants of exotic tribes. A man in a blue jellaba and a white skull cap is shaping the various colored babouches, made from the leather we saw drying on the walls and terraces of Fez.

Colors seep into your consciousness as never before: a sky-blue jellaba with a black face veil, a pearl-grey jellaba with a yellow veil, a black jellaba with a red veil, a shocking-pink jellaba with a purple veil. The clothes conceal the wearers' figures so that they remain elusive, with all the intensity and expression concentrated in the eyes. The eyes speak for the body, the self, for the age, conveying innumerable messages from their deep and rich existence.

After color and the graceful sway of robes, the flares, the stance, the swing of loose clothes, come the odors. One stand is devoted to sandalwood from Indonesia and the Philippines. It lies in huge round baskets and is sold by weight, for it is a precious luxury wood for burning as incense. The walls of the cubicle are lined with small bottles containing the essence of flowers—jasmine, rose, honeysuckle, and the rose water that is used to perfume guests. In the same baskets lie the henna leaves that the women distill and use on their hair and hands and feet. For the affluent, the henna comes in liquid form. And there is, too, the famous *kohl*, the dust from antimony that gives the women such a soft, iridescent, smoky radiance around their eyes.

The smell of fruit, the smell of perfumes, and the smell of leather intermingle with the smell of wet wool hanging outside of the shops to dry—gold bedspreads hanging like flags in the breeze, sheep's-wool rugs, the favored cherry-red wool blankets, and rose carpets, like fields of daisies, lilies, apple blossoms. Blue is the symbolic color of Fez, a sky blue, a transparent blue, the only blue that evokes the word long-forgotten and loved by the poets: azure. Fez is azure. You rediscover the word "azure."

The smell of cedar grows stronger. We are now in the carpenters' quarter. It is spacious, high enough for the beams of wood, brought by the donkeys, to be turned into tables, chairs, trunks. The smell is delicious, comparable only to that of fresh-baked bread. The wood is blond, and the carpenters work with care and skill. The art of working mother-of-pearl encrustations is rare. Two members of the distinguished family that alone knows the art are teaching it to children. I watch them work in the aisle of the museum, with pieces as tiny as one-eighth of an inch, shaping and fitting them to a sculptured rosewood box. It is not an art found in tourist bazaars. To watch hands at such delicate work is to understand the whole of the Moroccan character—patience, timelessness, care, devotion.

And now we are in the street of spices. They look beautiful in their baskets, like an array of painter's powders. There is the gold-red saffron, the silver herbs, the scarlet-red peppers, the sepia cinnamon, the ochre ginger, and the yellow curry. The smells surround you, enwrap you, drug you. You are tempted to dip your whole hand in the powdery colors. Later these herbs and spices will appear subtly in the local cooking.

The Moroccan can work in a small space because he knows the art of stillness, he is concentrated on his work, immobile. He does not know restlessness. He is unravelling silk skeins, rolling the silk onto bobbins, tying and braiding belts. But just as you begin to float on a dream of silk, muslins, embroidery, you are plunged into the hundreds of hammer blows of copperwork. Copper trays, copper-edged mirrors, candelabra, tea pots, are being carved with a burin and hammer. The men hold the large trays between their knees. The oldest and the best of the artists works with infinite precision, reproducing designs from famous mosques. His dishes shine like gold, and the designs open and flower and expand and proliferate like intoxicated nature. There are always children and young men in the background, learning the craft.

After the roar of copper works, the hammer strokes, comes a different tone of clatter. It is the work on pewter, iron cauldrons for laundry, pots and pans for cooking.

The barber shop is a mysterious cavern, with four huge thronelike chairs taking the whole space. In ancient times the barber was also the circumciser and sometimes the surgeon.

Children pass by, giggling and running, carrying trays of dough prepared for the communal oven. Every quarter has its own mosque, its fountain, its school, its *hammam*, or bath, and its communal oven. The little girls of five and six carry the baby of the family tied to their backs with shawls. They manage to play in between their duties.

A small stand sells sugar loaves—the gift to bring when invited to dinner—sugar for the mint tea and for the sweet pastry, so flaky and light, that they bake.

Two women pass me in gold and silver caftans, on their way to a party or a wedding.

The only sights I miss from my former visit, many years ago, are the handsome cavaliers in their full regalia, white burnouses, red trimmings on the horses, gold knives in their belts. The rich families of sheiks have gone to live in Casablanca. So all I see now are donkeys and mules laden with wood for burning, with dried skins, with furniture, with fruit and garbage, with bolts of material, with potato sacks, with bricks. And when they come with a shout of warning you have to squeeze yourself against the walls.

Now we come to the dyers' souk. The whole crooked, serpentine street of cobblestones belongs to them, and your foot discovers first of all a river of colored water overflowing from the vats. The guide says: "Don't mind. Your shoes will be dyed in beautiful colors." In every dark cavernous lair there are cauldrons with dyes of different hues. The men dip the wool and silk and then squeeze them dry. Their legs are bare, and both legs and hands are dyed the color they work with. Children are watching, learning, and helping when they can.

Glancing into one mosque, discreetly, I see a sumptuous blood-red rug given by the king. There is a separate prayer room for the women. Before entering, the faithful wash their feet and faces at the fountain.

Mosques, markets, souks, schools, baths, are all intertwined, giving a feeling of common humanity, or intimacy. Every trade is carried out in the open. Passing by the schools I hear the chorus of recitation from the Koran, which children learn at the earliest age. Wooden trellised windows conceal them from the street, but some come to the door to smile. Learning the verses by heart is difficult, and the discipline severe.

There are no schools for women, but they learn their arts and crafts from the skilled workers who serve them: dressmaking, embroidery, painting, pottery, weaving. Their knowledge is not confined to housekeeping. In ancient days they excelled in poetry, philosophy, and music.

Inevitably the rug merchant invites you to drink mint tea and to glance at the rugs. They are spread on the floor of an ancient palace, now a warehouse for rugs. You learn to distinguish between the designs of Fez and the Berber. The Fez recall the flowery, intricate designs of Persia, but the Berber rugs, in natural wool with austere, abstract designs in pure colors, recall American Indian patterns in their simplicity.

The old inns, or *fondouks*, are still there, as they were in the Middle Ages. Donkeys and camels rest in the courtyard, and in the cells all around, the merchants who come from other cities sleep in their burnouses. But many of the inns have been turned over to the craftsmen and artisans. One is filled with sheepskins, which are being dipped in lye to make it easier to pull off the wool.

A heavy cedarwood gate, elaborately carved, with a heavy silver lock or a tree-sized bolt, indicates a wealthy home.

In a dark lair men are feeding the fires for the hammam, throwing into the furnaces chips left over from carpentry or bundles of odorous eucalyptus.

Baskets of mint are sold in abundance, sometimes by one solitary old woman. When I stop at a very small and dark café, I see the samovar they keep going, and watch the ritual of making mint tea. I sit on a plain rough bench, and the boy in charge of pressing the mint into the tea pot brings a tiny stool for the glasses.

The tall red hat the Moroccans love to wear, with its black tassel, came from Turkey and is called a *tarbouche* by the natives, a *fez* by the tourists.

I say to a merchant, persistently pointing inside his shop, which is filled with antiques: "I am not shopping. I am writing about Fez." He bows and replies in flowery French, "Come in for the pure delight of the eyes."

For the pure delight of the five senses!

The strong pungent smell of tanning is the only unpleasant one. Tanning occupies a whole square all to itself, with immense vats holding a cement-colored liquid. The men work half-naked, using hooks to handle the skins. Eight or ten vats are worked at the same time, and the skins hung on the wall to dry.

Knowing that Fez—one of Morocco's Four Imperial Cities—was the center of religious and cultural life from ancient times, I want to visit the library of the Karaovine University, which contains original Arabic manuscripts. For this visit I am given a guide called Ali. He is tall, handsome, dark-haired, with an olive complexion, and he speaks French with beautiful diction. He is dressed in the traditional brown jellaba and pointed yellow slippers. I know the Arabian love of poetry, the cult of the spoken word, the gift for storytelling. Ali transports me to the year 900 by his recitation of verses from the Koran, his chanting of the poetry of Omar Khayyam. He is deeply concerned about the survival of Fez. He shows me the exquisite students' quarters, those which were opened and reconstructed by the Beaux Arts. But he also shows me those which have been condemned for lack of repairs, with their sad, plain wood bolts drawn tight, and those which have been put to other uses such as the carving of cedarwood by an artist. He shows me the neglected fountain with the tile decoration partly eroded. He makes me fearful that this vision of other centuries might vanish, like a dream out of *A Thousand and One Nights*, through carelessness or indifference. He wants America the bountiful, America the rebuilder of Versailles, to intervene, to rescue the sculptured cedar beams, the subtle tile work, the lace patterns of the stucco, the delicate arches. In between his canto to the beauty of Fez, so much more refined, so much more intellectual, so much more spiritual than other cities, and his canto to its skilled artisans, Ali recited verses from Omar Khayyam:

> Lo! Some we loved, the loveliest and best
> That Time and Fate of all their Vintage prest,
> Have drunk their Cup a Round or two before,
> And one by one crept silently to rest.

He makes me aware of the fragility of Fez, that we should see it well before it vanishes, that we should learn the myriad gestures of its craftsmen's hands, their patience, their delight in transforming every stone, every piece of wood, every layer of stucco, into an object of beauty. He makes me lament the corroded woods, the broken tiles, the neglected palaces abandoned to time, and the fig tree cut down in the square in front of the library where the students once gathered for discussions, to read their poems and pin them to the tree for passers-by to judge.

The treasure of the library, the illuminated manuscripts, are locked away from my eyes, but Ali is a living spokesman for all I have read about Fez. His softly modulated voice comes from the intellectual and literary past of luminous Fez.

He reminds me of a storyteller I had seen in Fez years before. Ali says he will not be there in the winter. The square where sword swallowers, water carriers, rug sellers, dancers, acrobats, and storytellers gathered is too cold and no place to linger in. But I am stubborn, and on Friday, the Islamic holiday, I go to the square. Even though it has only fifty or a hundred visitors, I find my storyteller standing in the center of an attentive, rapt group of listeners of all ages. They squat on the ground, absolutely absorbed by him, not wavering in their attention for one moment. He is young, wears a heavy wool jellaba of black and white stripes, and a white skull cap, and he carries a stick for emphasis. He has huge glowing eyes, a swarthy skin, and regular features. He is telling the story of Ali Baba with dramatic emphasis, with suspenseful pauses, with a flowing, incantatory style.

Because of Ali's emphasis on the ephemeral beauty of Fez and the possibility of its vanishing, my recurrent feeling that I am dreaming within other centuries, I seek with even more intensity to hold this dream close at least during my stay. I see the tiles broken into small pieces for the mosaic work, I see the lightness and clarity of the air, I see the old ramparts, the city's walls, covered with soft verdigris, lichen, and moss. The secret essence of Fez is serenity. It is expressed in its stillness at night, the rare lights, in the tamarisk trees that never look dishevelled, in the figures stirred by the wind, in Cézanne blues, Dufy pinks, pearl whites, and charcoal blacks. The secret essence of Fez comes to me at five-thirty in the morning when I awaken to the *muezzin*, the prayer call, from the minaret. Five times a day this prayer is chanted; it seems like both a lament and an invocation, a consolation and a lyrical thanksgiving. At five-thirty in the morning it takes on a special quality, that of a lonely faith protecting the sleeping city, a prayer which is also a call to awaken those prodigious, dynamic hands, agile and supple, never still and never lazy, resting only at the moment of prayer.

It is Ali who tells me the legend of the name of Fez. It had its inception in the democratic spirit of the founder, Idriss II. When the site was chosen and building began, the king took a pick and gave the first stone-breaking blow. The word for pick was *fez*. During later excavations a gold pick was found, said to have been given to the founder as a symbol. When this legend is questioned, museum keepers are apt to answer with silence—respect for legends being as great as respect for fact.

Ali is not content with quoting Omar Khayyam and the Koran, but he recites his own poetry, poems to the beauty of Fez, naming its trees—araucaria, ginger, bamboo, date, monkey puzzle; its fruit; its flowers.

He has theories about visitors. They should not be treated as tourists. They should be invited as friends to weddings, funerals, birthdays, and feast days.

This makes me accept the invitation of the waiter at the Palais Jamai, who says his wife wants to cook a real couscous for me. We go to a tiny house, climb tiny stairs, and find her cooking in a tiny kitchen on the terrace. She is beautiful, with large eyes and a noble profile. She has been cooking all day. I sit in the living room, with its low divans all along the wall and the round copper table in the center. On the walls hang the blue Fez pottery dishes. Cookies are brought in, made like the domed pewter dish I saw being shaped in the souks. The wife's mother is visiting. She comes from the north. Neither woman speaks French, but we manage to convey friendliness, and I show my appreciation of the couscous, which is delicious: a mound of millet, saffron-colored, topped by vegetables, chicken, and raisins. We eat from the same dish. The mother's hands are hennaed, and I notice she is not eating. When I ask Mr. Lahlou why, he explains she cannot eat with spoon and fork. So I say we are the clumsy ones who do not know how to eat with our hands. Then the mother eats, skillfully and neatly, making little balls out of the millet. The meal ends with a large sweet orange, which the host peels and shares with all. And, of course, mint tea. When I am about to leave, the host takes down from the wall the blue pottery dishes and gives them to me. He explains that the tourists are not properly welcomed. The ancient ideal of hospitality is still in evidence. Hospitality is sacred among the people of Islam.

On this day of no wind the smoke of the communal ovens can be seen from the window of the hotel, a clean white smoke. And on such days the five golden balls on the tip of the minarets, symbolizing the five prayers, shine like suns.

When two little boys quarrel in the souks, wrestling angrily, Mustafa, the guide, not only separates them but insists they kiss each other's hair. The men greet each other also with a kiss on the hair when they meet in cafés, and hold hands in the streets as they talk. The whole of life exudes a fraternal tenderness.

"Now when it was the thousand and first night, Dunyayad said to her sister . . ."

Morocco

At the Club Méditerranée in Moorea, we were really in Tahiti. But at the club in Agadir, Morocco, we are in a French pension. Arabs are not invited. Agadir, after the earthquake which razed it, is all new. The chef de village was a chef de village from a French suburb. The curse of rock-and-roll is not limited to the pool and dining room, for the loud-speakers are set far from the club, to its very edges, to reach every cottage. The architecture is Moroccan, but that is all. The pool is like a pool in Paris or Long Island, the rock-and-roll spoils the meals. The sea is ice cold. The only solution is to travel, to go on tours, and then it is wonderful. We leave early on a Land Rover, with a young French college student as a guide. We drive into the Atlas Mountains in southern Morocco, to solitary mountain towns with houses built out of the red earth. We drive through mountains and flatlands and sand dunes, often without roads. After hours of dust, dry air, extreme heat, we get desperately thirsty, and only then does one understand the deep beauty of an oasis. The green, the fruit, the shade, the water. There are rivulets in which we bathe our feet, fountains at which we drink. After the desert, the

From the diary of Anaïs Nin.

trees seem a hundred times greener, the water a hundred times fresher. At one place lunch is served under a tent. The ground is covered with rugs. The tables are copper trays on mother-of-pearl bases. The lamb on a spit is brought whole and we eat with our fingers. Couscous has a golden color. For dessert we have figs and sweet tea. Another time, after a long desert drive, we arrive at dusk at Ouarzazate where we find a beautiful hotel belonging to the Club, native architecture, a sober castle of red earth. A fountain, high and wide, falls from the wall into the pool. A baby antelope greets us and then returns to her bed of straw in the open fireplace. The dining room is below the pool, and as we dine we can see the swimmers like fish in an aquarium. The rooms are named after minerals: Azurite, Serpentine, Quartz, Onyx, Alabaster, Calcite. This is the land of minerals. Children see them on the road, exhibited on tables or sometimes, if they are small pieces, inside of bottles.

The view from the bedroom is a never-ending desert colored a delicate sepia or mauve with silver-grey bushes. The endlessness gives a feeling of infinity. In infinity both death and life are suspended. It is a moment of freedom from both. The air is clear, pure. The silence is soothing, matching the space. Facing us is the walled-in city used in films. One film company has reconstructed the gate.

I want to stay here. I love the women so mysteriously wrapped in black, their rhythmic walk, their proud carriage as they carry their jugs on the way to the fountain. I love the jewelled eyes from behind veils, the children with a beauty so vivid, so dazzling. I love the men, austere, violent, proud of bearing. In the evening the women dance, dressed in many layers of pastel-colored chiffon and layers of jewels. The men ride and shoot long, old-fashioned rifles in the air. I love their secretiveness and their curiosity.

They watch us from the roofs of their houses. The windows are small, no more than half a yard high and twelve inches wide, like jail windows, intended to keep out the hot sun. They are grated too. We are allowed into one of the homes built into the hill like a prehistoric cave. The floor is of beaten earth, the shape follows the contours of the hill. On the left there is a dugout for the donkey, on the right a dugout for the baby asleep on a sheepskin. We walk uphill to the bedroom. A rug on the floor, one dress on a nail, one necklace. One holy picture from the Koran, which I have seen on sale in the market. On the corner is a site for the fire and a cauldron suspended over it. The whole place, carved into the earth, was built for shelter, shade, the earth walls and tiny windows keep the place cool and sunless. A life in the bower of the earth, in darkness. As we leave the place, we see that the husband is crippled and that he may allow the visitors in for the sake of a small donation.

I see the men threshing wheat as the Mexicans do, with their feet and the hoofs of horses. They sing as they work. They throw the wheat in the air to strain it, to the rhythm of their singing.

One morning at dawn we go to the camel market at Goulimine on the edge of the Sahara Desert. This is in the region described as the Blue Arabs. The caftans are all in special shades of blue worn by no other tribe. The dye ultimately tints their skin blue, and so they are called the Blue People. The camels are of all sizes and qualities. There is much bargaining and examining of the camels' teeth for age.

The eyes of young and old are always fiery. The eyes of the children burn like sun reflected on onyx.

We are living in Biblical times. There is no change. The children will be corrupted by the tourists. They have

Morocco

133

learned to beg, even though their parents punish them for doing so.

One guide, in his immaculate blue caftan and stiff white shirt, demonstrates how he climbs a tree and cuts down a coconut without soiling or wrinkling his clothes.

There is always the smell of a wood they burn, which resembles the smell of incense. These lovely, quiet towns in the middle of the desert. The people are silent. There may be the sound of a small flute, the bells on an animal, a religious chant, which take on a sharpness against the silence, a silence we never know because of the multitude of sounds in our cities. People, animals, buildings, stand out vividly against sky and sand dunes, never to be erased from memory because of the slow rhythm, the arresting of attention, the wholeness of the vision not frittered away, shredded by chaos and confusion of our cities. I see the antelope, the children, the riders, the lamb on the spit, as we see the loved one distinct from the crowd.

I remember one night, in a Moroccan hotel built like a Spanish house around a courtyard. The stairs led to a terrace on the roof. I could not sleep. I walked about, went to the terrace. I heard the Moslem chant from the mosque. The stars seemed more numerous, as in Mexico, nearer. The town was asleep, all white and moonlit. That someone was praying for us while all were asleep made one feel mysteriously protected. Morocco spellbinds me again, as once before. It is a deep and undefinable attraction. I once thought it was the labyrinthine shape of its cities, but now I love the desert.

In Marrakesh I find the same intensity of life in the square as I did in Fez. The food stands, with the smell of cooking, the acrobats performing for attentive circles, the water-bearers dressed in medieval glitter with bells on their hats, the dancers leaping in the air, the sword swallowers astonishing the children, the fire swallowers, the rug merchants, the beggars, the veiled women, even the bedraggled hippies begging from the poor Arabs, counting on their religious sense of hospitality. I love the way they shelter themselves in their burnouses and fall asleep on doorsteps. It is hot. We sit on a terrace from which we can see the whole glittering spectacle. It is so rich in colors, smells, and sounds that one's hair tingles from the passionate intensity.

Coming out of a restaurant, late at night, we have to walk through narrow streets to meet our carriage at the square. The beggars rush at us. They are legless, armless, some on wheel chairs, some blind, some hunchbacked. It is an infernal scene. The eagerness, the rivalries, the thrust of their particular deformity inches from our eyes is Dantesque and terrifying. It is dark. The extreme form of their begging almost paralyzes compassion. One feels one has not enough to give, that they multiply, magnify, devour. There are too many to help. They follow us to the square. The gaiety of the restaurant, the dancing of the women in transparent muslins studded with gold beads, all this is erased by the beggars. The subterranean life of Morocco is tragic and gruesome.

One little Arab boy I remember particularly because he haunted the café, sat at everyone's table. He was seven or eight years old. He was beautiful but aware of it. He offered himself as a guide. He offered his sisters for sale, access to drugs. He knew a few phrases of English. He was glib, suave, full of charm, and corrupt.

The French guide is a young student, a descendant of George Sand. He has a feminine face, fluid and receptive. He loves Morocco and works hard at instilling respect in the visitors. But the other French tourists annoy me. They talk incessantly. Their trivial talk ruins the silence. It is futile and prevents them from seeing and feeling. When people's senses are receptive, there is silence. In the desert I felt my senses so alert that smells, and vibrations of air, and waves of unequal heat, and the tremble of leaves in the oasis, the coolness of the rivulets, seem to occupy all my attention. I feel like an animal, keen on the scent. I cannot understand the chatter and childish, noisy games such as throwing water on each other. I swear to return alone.

The birthday of the king brings festivities; the Arabs on horseback, rushing, galloping wildly and shooting as they gallop. The colorful, hypnotic dances. Tents have been erected, sensuous tents, black and white on the outside, but red inside. Rugs were laid on the ground. Copper trays are passed around with figs and cups of sweet mint tea. The riders are on the beach and we sit on the pier so that they fly towards us, silhouetted against sea and sky. The white horses and the white burnouses seem born from the foam of the waves. Their burning eyes against the white and the white against an incredibly blue sky.

Another day, another tent. A sumptuous dinner on the beach. The sides of the tents can be raised to let the breeze through. The fires of the roasting pit and the torches are sharp in the night.

The vivid beauty of Morocco is compelling and magnetic. Returning to our ugly cities, we remember Morocco as an oasis when you are thirsty for beauty.

Enchanted Places
136

The Spirit
of Bali

The dazzling physical beauty of Bali is an expression of its spirit.

It affects you from the moment you land in the soft climate, which prepares you to relax body and soul and fall into a rhythmic pattern like that of an underwater ballet.

The beauty of the people is universal; both men and women have flawless honey-colored skin, glossy black hair, and dazzling smiles. They wear colorful batiks tightly wound around the waist, down to the feet for the women and shorter for the men. As you drive to the hotel, the houses, both rich and poor, show the same stone wall covered with flowers and vines.

Taller than the walls are the family temples, pagodas with roofs of black thatch. In between the houses are the village temples for larger gatherings.

There are three thousand temples in Bali. Figures of many gods and goddesses ornament walls and gates, but the temples themselves are empty stages, awaiting sumptuous offerings from the people.

Gay colored pennants point the way to temples, to craft shops, to dances. They are made of palm leaves and often

From *The Village Voice*, 6 January 1975.

The Spirit of Bali

decorated with ribbons, flowers, shells. Other beckoning signs are bright festive umbrellas, once the privilege of priests only, in red, yellow, and blue with gold fringe.

The women, in orange sarongs, are small, perfectly moulded, with delicate hands and feet. Their voices are soft and have a chanting quality. A meal is served like a ritual, not to disturb the meditative, contemplative delights of the senses, drinking the smell of the sea, the velvet quality of the air, the smell of spices and flowers.

It is a land of few words, so that dreams are not shattered and dispelled. The Balinese believe that the nine months spent in the womb is a period of meditation. Everything is conducive to this flowering of the senses.

The beauty of the women, with their smooth skin, delicate soft features, graceful gestures; the charm of the houses, with the tips of small temples showing above the stone walls; the skillful and tasteful handicrafts; the sculptures on the temples, similar to the famous bas-relief of Cambodia and India; the intense colors of the rituals with accents on gold and orange, the opaline rice fields reflecting the skies in the sheet of water covering them—all this is permeated with meaning, with symbolic messages. That is why their work, their craft, their theater, and their music gives them joy. The first sight of a woman walking with sinuous steps, holding a basket on her head with her two arms curved like the handles of Greek vases, the grace and balance of unfaltering steps through mountain roads or rough terrain, is already an expression of their belief that physical balance creates inner balance, and that the evil spirits of illness or insanity can only enter and possess people who are out of balance.

There are suggestions of animism, of ancestor worship, of Buddhist faith in transmigration. The gods dwell in the volcanoes, and some in the depth of the sea. One must not travel too high or too deep.

Everyone has a natural courtesy, a natural smile. The word for foreigner is "guest," not, as in other countries, "outsider."

The Balinese have no word in their language for art or artist. Creativity is natural and widespread. It is a natural means of honoring the gods and serving the community. They are all artists in our sense. The fisherman may be the musician at night, the village girl working all day may be one of the sophisticated dancers. Art is craftsmanship, the trancelike state of creation is simply communion with the gods.

The harmony of Balinese life has been achieved, it is the expression of an attitude. It is not that they ignore the darker forces of life. They know well that the world is full of dangers. But gods can be propitiated by beautiful rituals, elaborate, decorated offerings, prayers, by dancing and music. The gods are human. They enjoy beauty, music, dances, the three thousand temples built for them, treasure houses of sculptures. The Balinese confront evil by exteriorizing it in distorted, frightening sculptures, familiar with their threatening, contorted angry faces, which they carve in masks. On the stage the witch, the evil god, never dies. The Balinese are realists, but they are artists in their expression of rituals and ceremonies. They reach peaks of aesthetic beauty unequalled even in Japan.

Dancing is not just an art form, it is an interpretation of life. Bali is the island of unending festivals, and dance and music are constant.

At ceremonies they dress with a taste for blending of colors which is faultless. The women use primary colors for their blouses, which they now wear because of the offensive stares and snickers of tourists. The sarong is in rich blends of colors and designs. The features of the Balinese are delicate, their eyes deep and brilliant. Their hands are finely shaped, even in the women who work. They adopted the bath towel to wind around on top of their heads as a cushion for the weights they carry.

They do not heat their meals. At any time, while at work, or by one of the little stands on the roadside, they open the carefully folded palm leaf and eat rice and a bit of chicken or fish. There is no slavery to the clock. If the men tire of work in the fields and are far from home, they build a small shed and sleep during the hottest hours of the day.

My guide is a young man from the university. He originally wanted to be a doctor but the studies took too long and the death of his father, shot by his best friend when they both worked on the police force, obliged Wayan Subudi to go to work early. He graduated in literature and might have been a writer but admits he is lazy. Subudi, with his Oriental slanted eyes, his good profile, his dazzling white teeth, his black softly curled hair, is an ideal guide. He possesses great knowledge of Bali but waits for questions, does not drown you in long speeches. He allows time for absorption, meditation, silences, and then when one asks a question he answers it simply and directly.

His brother runs a lime kiln (they crush and heat coral to make lime); his mother has a shop outside the compound in which they live. When I visit his home, he leads me to a simple whitewashed room with a window opening on rice paddies filled with ducks marching in formation. He shows me photographs of his relatives, of his father's cremation ceremony (the cost of which left the family penniless). When I first come in, the mother is in the open building cooking over a brasero.

He intimates that the university dissipated many of their beliefs but did not affect their sobriety (no drinking of alcohol, no overeating, no drugs). What other youths seem to obtain from drugs, they obtain by fasting and meditation.

He wants to know if I believe in transmigration. I say, "I wish I did."

He translates some of the signs in the temples. Some forbid women to enter during menstruation. Others forbid entrance unless one wears the sarong and headgear appropriate to the place. He permits me to rest, sitting on one of the walls, and later tells me it is forbidden as it is a sacred wall. He is like the spirit of Bali itself, like the bamboo xylophone, delicate and muted, resigned to working for his family. I give him a diary book to write in. His gentleness and soft way of imparting knowledge stays with me.

Everything about Bali stays with you. It is made of aesthetic and spiritual elements that touch something far deeper than the eyes. It is like the temple incense which clings to your clothes.

Each day Subudi takes me on a different voyage. In the daytime, the voyage is through villages, rice paddies, rain forests, mountains, volcanoes, lakes, temples. These intricate explorations through unmarked roads can only be done with a guide. Subudi always knows the historical, religious, or cultural significance of each sight.

We begin a journey of immersion in temples. Nehru called Bali the habitat of the gods. In ancient history it was described as "The Morning of the World." Each temple has a different spiritual dedication. They are usually composed of several towering pagodas, topped by black thatch roofs. They are empty stands for the reception of offerings. The women come in dazzling costumes, carrying offerings on their heads. These are sometimes two feet tall, a pyramid of fruit, flowers, mirrors, plaited bamboo shaped like flowers, birds, feathers, bows. They are artfully composed. The fruit and food lie there while they pray, surrounded by their children. During that time the god is said to absorb the spirit of the nourishment, and then the women can take the food home.

The Sea God Temple, Tanah, was built on a very small island and looks like a ship made out of rock. The black pagoda rises in silhouette against the sky. The tide is high but the women who bring offerings persist in walking into the water, which comes up to their hips. A rope has been strung on poles all the way to the island so they will not be swept away.

Many temples, many gods. Gods for the sea, valley, rice crops, fertility. Taman Ayun is surrounded by a moat which reflects the flowers and trees. Metal spikes, three-pronged like Neptune's trident, are planted at the tip of the roof to frighten evil spirits. On feast days the offering stand is covered with a rug. Umbrellas and offerings surround the priests. Some temples are built by several families, joining their fortunes to build individual temples to their ancestors under the shadow of the Mother Temple.

The Bat Cave Temple is a huge natural rock cave to which thousands of bats cling, waiting for the night, when they forage for fruit. These are sacred bats. The women sit cross-legged by their offerings. If they are praying they are also observing other visitors and keeping a watchful eye over their children. One young woman is breast-feeding her child. The pandanus leaf, out of which they fashion so many offering designs, shines with a transparent golden tone in the sun.

The volcano erupted in 1963. The first time, its lava flow stopped just before engulfing the temple, and people felt the gods had control of fire from the earth. But the second time, it engulfed the temple. The people quietly decided the offerings had been insufficient.

You can walk for hours through fields, forests, mountain roads as carefully tended as private gardens. In your mind's eye you will always see the tangerine, the violet, the green sarongs, the honey-colored skins, the black hair against a background of luxuriant greens. Some golden greens with the sunlight washing them, some glowing with dew or with water from a waterfall, or the gentle cascades of the rice paddies flowing from the terraced fields. So much dewy green fills one's lungs with a mysterious oxygen. The walk of the old people, never stiff or brittle, reveals that their aging process does not deprive them of flexibility and grace. They do heavy work, ploughing, pounding, threshing, carrying weights and sheaves of rice or stones for the road. But it is all done with a natural rhythm, as they walk for miles, a rhythm never broken, no haste, no tensions, no driving force whipping them beyond their natural energy.

In the gentle rain, the scene changes. They use a date palm leaf for a head cover; our umbrellas are black, but theirs, canary yellow, shocking pink, tangerine, and lime.

I visit the instrument maker, who is highly respected in the community. Much formal bowing and many courtesies exchanged. On the right is an open-pit forge with three men working the bellows, where the metal is shaped. In other open buildings men are squatting, sculpturing the wood ornamentation of the *g'nder*, a musical instrument. In still another building instruments are painted and gilded. The big gong, which the instrument maker demonstrates, pounds on the heart, vibrates through the body.

The oldest village in Bali was isolated for a long time; it did not mingle with the other villages. It stands now as an austere example of simplicity. The stone houses were built in a uniform line on each side of a wide cobblestone road. A long shed with a raised platform, with a roof of sugar palm fiber and lit by an oil lamp, serves as a meeting place for the elders. Few belongings, few furnishings, no clutter; a loom, an ancient instrument, photographs of ancestors, a mat to sleep on. The elders dispense law and justice, set dates for rituals. The scribe, as he is called, sits cross-legged near the entrance of the village, carving mythological stories in Sanskrit and illustrating them. He engraves on palm leaves an inch and a half wide and twelve inches long, which are then tied together by a piece of bark and are meant to be opened like an accordion.

In Bali you are not judged by your possessions (they are contemptuous of wealth); you are judged by your manners and your hierarchy in the spiritual and artistic world. The musician, the dancer, the mask maker, the wood carver, the stone carver, are respected, for art is man's tribute to the gods; every craft is sacred and meaningful.

Day and night the air is vibrant with what Colin McPhee, the composer, described as the golden metallic sound of the gamelan, a rain of silver. In the daytime there are rehearsals for the night. Exciting, striking at every cell, the sequined sound of the gamelan is like a multitude of bells. The wistful flutes rise above the metallic g'nder, and the ensemble is punctuated by the deep throb of the gongs. The animation comes from the multiple metal rain.

At night the villages are filled with music. Each village has its orchestra of gamelan players. There are dances in hotels, in village community buildings. All the natives, from the smallest child to the oldest grandmother, come to watch. It is their delight, these recurrent stories from India's mythology, legends they know by heart. As in Japanese theater, it is not the story which concerns them, but the variations in the performances, and they come and go as if music and dance were an accompaniment to their life, not a spectacle, as natural as the breeze from the sea, the murmuring of trees, the pendulum sway of the banyan lianas.

The dancers are tightly bound in hand-woven scarves of many colors mixed with glittering gold or silver threads. Most of the motion comes from the hands, arms, and feet. The body contributes an undulation, like a wave, which arches the back and thrusts the breasts and the hips out. A fan in each hand, held high under the armpits, the dancers flutter continually to suggest the wings of a hummingbird. They dip and whirl, skimming the ground like swallows, shifting their heads from left to right as if they would separate from their bodies. The colors of sarongs, scarves, and headgear are so rich that one must see the same dance several times to become aware of the layers of textures and combinations of tones.

The headdresses of the dancers are triangular frameworks, sometimes painted on thin white wood, sometimes made of gold or silver filigree, sometimes inlaid with jewels or mother-of-pearl or a mixture of the velvet-white frangipani flowers and one red hibiscus in the center. In poor villages they turn to inventive substitutes. Covarrubias, the Mexican painter, once saw on a dancer's tiara an advertisement with a yellow globe floating languidly among degrees of latitude and longitude, which from afar looked very decorative.

In Bali, color has significance, as does everything the Balinese use. In the Mother Temple, black is for Vishnu, white is for Siva, and red for Brahma. Every gesture of the hands has a symbolic meaning. The arabesque of head and shoulders has a meaning. The puppet show, so dear to the Balinese, is meaningful.

The magically powerful shadow play is not only the first

ancestor of Balinese theater, it is also the first expression of the Balinese belief in the reality of the symbol, and the first lesson to the child in the reality of the symbol. It signifies that our life is a shadow play, that man himself is a shadow of god.

The puppets are cut from buffalo hide, then painted, then stiffened with glue. The stems are made from buffalo horns, colored with the juice of plants. The puppeteer sets up his stand in the village and everyone soon knows he is there. He sits behind a screen. An old and smoky oil lamp hangs over him but is bright enough to create the shadows he wants. Tiny boy apprentices sit cross-legged around him, ready to hand him the puppets he needs. His art consists not only of moving the puppets according to the story but giving each one a different voice. The quality of the voice is unreal; the intonations very similar to those in Japanese Noh plays.

The people watch these stories for hours; Westerners rarely can.

To see the shadows talking, fighting, flying, loving, in the emollient Balinese night is stirring enough, but to steal behind the screen and watch the beauty of the puppets, their intricate costumes, embroideries, ornaments, is even more impressive; to see the children so familiar with the characters that they know which one comes next; to see the man sitting cross-legged like the storytellers of old, under the trembling oil lamp, swelling up for the big voices, shrinking for the women's voices, is to be carried back centuries into the depths of India from which came the Balinese mythology, religion, and theater.

Covarrubias, who lived in Bali, stressed the color of these events and described them as "a pageant that would have made Diaghilev turn green with envy."

Covarrubias felt that the most charming quality of the

Balinese is this happy combination of primitive simplicity and highly refined art. They retain a close contact with the soil, live practically out of doors in simple thatched houses, walls of split bamboo, cool mats for sleeping, using artifacts belonging to a primitive culture, tools made of bamboo, wood, light but strong baskets, clay vessels to keep the water cool, bamboo water pipes, bamboo for their instruments, altars, sun hats, fans. But for their rituals, dances, and temple offerings they demonstrate an art in costume and decoration, in dramatic effects, background, in theatrical atmosphere which is unequalled.

The colors, the perfumes, the dances, the music of Bali, stay with us because they all penetrate deep into our psychic life; it is one of the bardo states we are allowed to live, a privilege, a voyage through a karma of joy not granted to Western man, a joy which comes from shared work and symbolic oneness with nature, with religion, and with other human beings. We could not create this, but it was given to us as an offering, perhaps with the message "Do not corrupt it."

Port Vila,
New Hebrides

The approach to an island is always a reawakening of childhood expectations about islands. From our reading, islands were the undiscovered, the mysterious, the isolated, the unfamiliar.

Port Vila, on the island of Efate, has a history which appeals to the imagination. It was first discovered by Captain Cook, then later by the sandalwood seekers. The Chinese paid high prices for this fragrant wood, which was used for religious ceremonies. The search for sandalwood was like the American gold rush until the island was quickly depleted of its sandalwood trees. Then came the whalers, the missionaries, the colonizers. All of them were exposed to cannibalism as the native Melanesians hungered for sources of protein.

Seen from the plane, the tropical verdure presents infinite variations of green, from gold-yellow to the darkest shade, and it is difficult to remember that it is described as an island of ashes and coral, subject to erosion by the sea. Remembering this gives a mood of fleeting beauty to the island, as if we must love it in the present.

At the airport there are two customs lines, each headed

From *Travel & Leisure*, November 1975.

by gigantic blue-black Melanesians in tropical uniforms, French for one line, British for the other. Then I remember that the New Hebrides islands are run jointly by England and France as a condominium, referred to by the locals as a pandemonium.

Driving to the hotel through the rain forest, one sees the first curtains of lianas, masses of ferns, the breadfruit tree with its spatulated leaves, the banyan tree, ever-present in fairy tales, because of its spreading roots, convoluted like giant human hands or like the long fingers of witches, grasping the earth, encroaching, invading, and throwing massive shadows and strangling vines into our dreams.

Not as many flowers as Tahiti, not as many birds or animals, more like an ocean of striated leaves, some as large as elephant ears. What emanates from the island is tranquility, remoteness. There is in us a hunger for remoteness. It places a great distance between our preoccupations. The island makes the break with the mainland of our concerns. There we are, adrift in a new world. The stillness is soothing, the lagoon is tranquil with all the colors of the opal stone.

The New Hebrides have several variants of a myth which may demonstrate they did not wish to be an island. They claim that Maui, the hero who fished up their island, also fished up Australia, and if his line had not broken, they would still be joined.

The Hotel Le Lagon was built on the best site of the island between rolling hills and a beautiful protected lagoon surrounded by tropical rain forest. Separate bungalows, built like native huts, melt into the brown of tree trunks, into the vegetation. They have roofs thatched of palm leaves, plaited wild cane on the walls, supports of kohu trunks—a wood unique to Port Vila.

I was told I could walk along the beach of fine coral

sand, shaded by casuarina branches, to the Museum of Oceanic Art established by Nicolai Michoutouchkine. I had already been initiated to some of this striking collection at the Maeva Beach Hotel in Tahiti and the Hotel Château Royal in Noumea. But these great pieces are not in their element in hotel lobbies. Here, as I arrive by way of the beach, the sculptures suddenly tower twelve feet high out of Michoutouchkine's tropical garden, carved out of huge tree trunks, slit down the middle to be used as drums, but ending at the tip with powerful gods' faces. They become presences out of the past which can never be erased from memory. The first sight of these sculptures gives to the early part of the trip a strong flavor of past cultures, a past of people who could sculpture gods out of trees.

Standing with a group of gods among the trees and bushes are Michoutouchkine and Pilioko, the most famous painters of the region, known for their own work and for the collection Michoutouchkine has spent so much love and care upon. Pilioko wears a colorful sarong, a shirt, bracelets of shark bones; he is tall and lean, with enormous, soft, dark eyes and features drawn with power. His later works are embroidered tapestries featuring animals, people, flowers, and trees interwoven in a mythical, abstract style of his own. Michoutouchkine wears a chieftain's robe; he has short hair, lively humorous eyes, a warm smile, and the sturdy body we associate with Russian origins. He goes to sleep at sundown like the natives, is up at sunrise. He has no need of a telephone, electric lights, newspapers, or radio. The group of buildings is artistic and simple. One closed house serves as living quarters and Pilioko's studio; the rest are open thatch-roofed buildings housing the collection and the paintings and tapestries. Extensions and sheds were added as the collection grew.

Enchanted Places
150

Pilioko is a Polynesian from Wallis Island; two other young men, Joel and George, are from the Solomons. Freddy is a boy from the "small nambas" tribe on Malekula Island in the New Hebrides. They are all preparing a Polynesian lunch in a pit nearby; I can see the smoke issuing from the hot stones.

It is difficult to concentrate on the collection because it is interesting to talk with both Nicolai and Pilioko. Pilioko's presence is vivid, Nicolai is the eloquent one. A book should be written about Nicolai. When he finished his studies at the Sorbonne, he went off without a penny on a journey that was supposed to last six months (the first hitchhiker before it became popular). He stayed away twenty years. He has been all over the world, a man who travelled with love, who was no tourist, who entered deeply into the life of each country, learned the language, painted, sketched, absorbed, gave exhibitions. He began to collect Oceanic art, finally gathering five thousand pieces, weighing twelve tons, of a craft and art which might have been obliterated. Now, most of this collection is continually travelling to give it maximum exposure to people of the South Pacific and other parts of the world. Nicolai has a passion for art and a genius for friendship. He is truly described by the French word *formidable*. (Once he talked the crew of a French destroyer into transporting items he had collected on a distant island thousands of miles to the Museum at Port Vila.) He can speak all the languages and dialects of the various tribes and has used this to advantage in his collecting throughout the South Pacific Islands. As he collected, he also set up exhibitions in plazas and churchyards of little island hamlets. The response of the natives was amazing; either they knew the artifacts displayed, or some racial memory enabled them to respond to the symbols of their roving Pacific ancestors. Now

Michoutouchkine, understanding the intermingling of races and arts among the different islands, insists that the collection be united as Oceanic art.

The collection deserves a life study. It reveals exquisite craftsmanship in wood, shells, tapa cloth, coconut fiber. Masks, animals, birds, gods, are skillfully sculptured, and as much art is spent upon fishing implements, agricultural tools, baskets, cloths, combs, necklaces, headgear, and weapons. Every object made for use is decorated, embellished, enhanced.

Michoutouchkine's own paintings are either strong, bold studies of native heads, or groups of figures in dense, diffused tones. Pilioko is justly considered as Oceanic Picasso because he has extracted from his native Polynesian background a decorative, abstract, modern essence.

The living quarters themselves are a museum of another kind. Pilioko has hung on the walls, on the ceilings, over the banister, mementoes of their voyages: prayer rugs from Tibet, scarves from India, coins, Berber mats, Portuguese earrings, New Guinea masks, tapa from Fiji, whales' teeth, petrified bats, shell necklaces. As a dramatic climax, Nicolai opens a trunk containing his diaries, a treasure trunk, enough to entertain for a thousand and one nights! We talk of travels, people, art. He describes the museum he wants France to build. He has offered his entire collection and the land he owns if they will erect a building. He is concerned that a hurricane might damage the fragile, open structure now housing the collection.

The lunch is cooking with unfamiliar pungent smells. The pit is covered with hot stones, and water sprinkled on them makes them steam. The food is wrapped in banana leaves. It has been sealed for three hours. Now the stones are being removed and the food is unwrapped and placed on hand-carved wooden trays four feet long. The bowls are carried to the long table facing the sea. The dishes are of carved wood in the shape of a turtle or a fish. As the inner banana leaves are opened there is poi, taro, bread-fruit, yams, crab, pig. A coconut sauce is passed in a bowl to be used on everything. There is wine. Before lunch a silver loving cup is passed around, filled with lime juice and pisco from Peru; later it is filled with champagne. The boys from other islands serve with gaiety. Nicolai is telling us that when he visited tribes to find pieces for his collection, the first test of his genuine friendship was to eat with them. Any sign of repulsion or indifference to their food was a sign of unfriendliness. Once he had to eat pancakes made by an old woman whose skin was in tatters. They watched him. He did not admit to having been ill. He knew the sharing of food was the symbol of fraternity.

The natives told Nicolai: There are four kinds of people who visit us—the administrator, the trader, the missionary, the ethnographer; but we never met a man like you that walks into our house and behaves like one of us. You are able to eat our food, sleep on the ground, to behave just as we do. We feel you must be one of us.

When Nicolai takes me on a tour of the island, I find that this is true. The natives build their huts inland, quite a distance from the road. You might not see them if you do not know where to look. Nicolai knows and suddenly darts into the woods, then beckons to me. As I approach, there is a complete Melanesian family sitting around a wood fire, which is cooking their meal. He purchases and gives me a basket which has been hanging in their hut over the smoke. It is black and smells of many foods.

He knows their songs: "Air me no save."

He knows how they describe a brassiere: "Basket belong titi."

He knows what they call the white man's saw: "Something belong white man you push em I go you pull em I come I save kai kai wood."

He knows the definition of a piano in pidgin English: "Something belong white man em I got white tooth em I got black tooth you kill em I cry."

He knows of the rousette, called a flying fox by natives but really a bat. It feeds on fruit at night and is delicious to eat when it has fed on certain fruits.

We meet natives from other islands, Toara and Tongariki. We meet a Polynesian couple with children, the most beautiful of all. The man tall and proud, the woman with delicate Oriental features. He carries a machete and a basket of woven banana leaves. They are picking fruit and taro.

We see coconut trees with red bark, orange butterflies in droves, tropical trees in flamboyant orange, ironwood, and the tobacco tree, which contains an antidote for fish poisoning.

Most delightful are the tiny, untended roadside stands. Little thatch-roofed sheds offering melons, bananas, papaya, breadfruit, taro, fresh eggs, with the price of each item marked. You put the money in a box. In the old days they had a sign: "Don't cheat as God is watching you."

The ease with which Nicolai walks into their shacks, jokes and laughs with them in their own language, makes me understand why they relinquish their most sacred crafts to him.

One morning at 6:30 AM Nicolai comes to fetch me; there is something I must see. Outside his museum garden, industrious spiders have woven yards of the most delicate webs covering all the bushes, and the dew has turned them into fine threads of diamonds glittering in the early sunlight. The webs are intricate, spanning from branch to branch, creating inner rooms of jewelled castles, labyrinths, cellular interweavings as carefully patterned as lace, forming necklaces, pendants, trailing brides' veils which will soon vanish with the warmth of the sun. Nicolai does not want me to miss any of the wonders of Port Vila.

Every time I see the great drum statues, the hollow tree trunks ending in carved and painted faces of gods, I am reminded of Jerome Robbins' ballet "The Age of Anxiety," when the parents appear on incredible stilts and walk on stage just like these ancient gods, to frighten and intimidate. Here they seem more like guardians, with their hooked noses and immense popping eyes looking down on us as we pose for photographs. We photograph Pilioko and his tapestry; Nicolai and his painting of the heart of a jungle; an incredible bird carved of wood by a native, which has not only the swift cutting edge of flight but carries the head of a man half sculptured out of his belly; another bird with a man's face.

Nicolai, the artist and world traveller, effaces himself to present Port Vila with a tenderness for the place which is more contagious than any of the descriptions made by journalists, by art critics, by literary visitors. He is never detached from what he is showing me. One morning he takes me to the market early, before the sun is too hot. Here under the trees beside the main road, the native women have come to lay out their wares. The most intricate and beautiful sea shells lie on mats. Coconut shells carved into cups. Fruits and flowers arranged as if they were colors for a painting, composed, layered, with a sense of design. Flowers are arranged with the art of a Matisse or of a Japanese flower arranger. Crabs are tied and are foaming at their plight. The women wear short mumus of bright flower patterns, the colors fusing with the colors of flowers and vegetables and fruit. Their muscles are relaxed like those of dancers about to sway; they move lightly even when fat. They sit under umbrellas. They wear bands around their foreheads similar to those worn by American Indians. The very old women do not disintegrate, they age like wood carvings, veined and wrinkled but their features intact, set in a mould of dignity. Many are stringing shells for the necklaces they sell, necklaces which, as in Tahiti and Hawaii, are tokens of greeting, welcome, friendship. Nicolai is shopping; he carries a basket made of soft green palm leaves neatly plaited and with a handle of coconut fiber braided for strength.

Once more, to give me the flavor of the island, Nicolai takes me to the best sea food restaurant, the Houstalet. The choicest sea food is served on a large platter. One of the specialties is a pâté of coconut crab liver, as delicate as pâté de fois gras. The meal ends with a special drink, apple calvados and mint, invented by Michoutouchkine.

I listen to his plans for the Museum of Oceanic Art. I leave wishing the museum might be built soon, so that one might visit Port Vila as a charming, modern, uncrowded city on a tropical island, and as a voyage into the past of Oceania.

The most fortunate event in travelling is to meet someone immersed in the life of a place, who loves it and lives in close communion with its inhabitants. Nicolai offered me the secret island of Efate, where shy and withdrawn natives would not otherwise have smiled. *Kousurata* in the native language means to travel, to roam. It is a tribute that, after all his wanderings, he should choose to rest and take root in Port Vila.

The Swallows
Never Leave
Noumea

From the plane you first notice soft, contoured, small islands, which seem to float along the coast of New Caledonia, and you remember the nostalgia of your youth for desert islands. Then some of the islands are no longer green, but become blue atolls, part of the barrier reef which creates the lagoons and protects undersea life; but these coral reefs can only live near the surface, so what lies below your plane is a carpet of opals, lapis lazuli, turquoise, of such beauty that an artist is said to have given up painting after seeing them. They are like artfully spilled pots of paint in all the colors of sea and sky plus the scintillating transparencies of jewels.

The nostalgia for desert islands is to be fulfilled by an abundance of empty beaches accessible only by boat, where those who love fishing can stop, cook their catch, and eat it with the freedom of a Robinson Crusoe.

Driving from the airport you notice new and strange species of trees, groves of niaouli (a eucalyptus whose bark is used for native huts) appearing like grotesque, gray giants, and Cook's pines, which Captain Cook loved, and whose straight trunks, often one hundred feet tall, he used

From *Westways*, January 1976.

to replace his ship's masts. New Caledonia was Captain Cook's discovery. It reminded him of his native country, Scotland, so named it New Scotland; but in the landscape I see only a softness of outline, undulating mountains, which the Melanesian name of Noumea, the capital city, suits so well.

Arriving at the modern Hotel Château Royal, the paradox which sharpens one's senses begins. In the lobby of the hotel are exhibitions of Oceanic art belonging to the collection of Nicolai Michoutouchkine. Dark, fearsome, towering figures carved out of tree trunks, sometimes out of banyan tree roots. Primitive gods, ten feet tall, dominating the lobby, asserting the presence of indigenous art. Surrounding this is a gay, sun-filled, athletic vacation land resembling an uncrowded Riviera. We are in French territory thousands of miles from France, but here is France's sophisticated cuisine, perfumes, chic clothes, French books. In the hotel, with the gods looking on, you can lead a Riviera life by the sea.

The entire island is surrounded by a great coral barrier reef, so snorkeling and skin diving are full of surprises and treasures. There are short trips on a glass-bottomed boat for those who like to do their snorkeling above the surface. There is a boat trip with a charming French captain past floating islands (reminding you of childhood desserts, îles flottantes) to a tiny desert island at the harbor entrance featuring a French "pique-nique" lunch with barbecued fish. On the island is an impressive lighthouse sent by Napoleon (some say by mistake to Port de France in Noumea instead of Fort de France on the other side of the world in Martinique).

Noumea is a contrast of old and new. Modern buildings and homes stand next to vestiges of early French colonial architecture, from diminutive workmen's houses of sand-colored wood and peaked red tin roofs, ending in the French lightning rod, to classical colonial mansions.

It is a satisfying cycle to emerge from a modern city—in which the air is crystal clear, the freshness exhilarating, the hills dotted with well-tended white villas built by the exploitation of nickel, which also filled the many small harbors with boats of all kinds and shapes—from this to the amazing life at the bottom of the sea. One can walk from the Hotel Château Royal to the aquarium.

The aquarium is unique in the world today. It was constructed seventeen years ago by two marine biologists (using their own funds), Dr. Catala and his wife, Dr. Catala-Stucki. They were attracted to Noumea by the abundance and variety of tropical fish and corals in the lagoons protected by the great barrier reef. Here the fish and corals and other sea life are kept in the same water they came from, in a totally natural environment (nothing in the tanks is inanimate), and nourished as they nourished themselves in the sea. The sea life lives longer in this environment (some fish have lived in the aquarium seventeen years), which has enabled the Catalas to do long-term studies. In one of these studies, they discovered the fluorescence of deepwater corals, revealing an unknown world, a world which shames the jewellers. Under ultraviolet light, corals, which ordinarily open to feed only at night, can be observed in their mysterious fluorescence, when they unfold and stretch their tentacles seeking nourishment. To see marine life in its natural environment was once only the privilege of deep-sea divers. Now scientists can make extended studies of corals, even watch one coral devour another when crowded, or observe the corals which move from place to place. This was first doubted by scientists, and Dr. Catala invited them to come and see. No one had known that corals have less weight in the sea because of their spongeous, air-filled sacs. Some corals are like flowers never seen before, only they palpitate. Some are set with tiny pearls and diamonds. Some are like curled white feathers or like snow-white petals set with opals and amethysts, while others are spiked round balls with five silver eyes and one red eye. The staghorn coral is chalk-white with black tips, the mushroom coral is lined with pale green. All eat plankton with constant, graceful dance motions, almost invisible undulations.

These are the treasures the courageous Catalas have brought to the surface for us. There were many obstacles to overcome. As the divers search for corals in the depths of the sea it is so dark and murky they often cannot find the basket used for transporting specimens, or the corals die in the process of moving, or the divers are stung by venomous polyps. "All these reefs," Dr. Catala writes, "are the site of luxuriant and diverse animal and plant life. This is where the enchantment of coral gardens is revealed . . . In the coral world everything is life and motion, light and color."

Back into a luminousness of perpetual spring—the swallows never leave Noumea—with lagoons and harbors filled with dancing boats, as Venetian canals are filled with dancing gondolas, to sinuous roads encircling the bays, tree-lined, uncrowded. The trees reach down to the beach. Four old men are playing boules, as they do in the south of France. A few plumes of orange smoke from the nickel factory appear but are carried away by the trade winds.

Long ago traders came here seeking sandalwood, then came whalers, then the missionaries. Finally France sent its political prisoners. One taxi driver remembers from his childhood the men wrapped in blankets, roaming the island looking for work, but more essential, for a family they could attach themselves to, work for, live with, to obtain the warmth lost by exile, the families and children lost by exile. He remembers being pampered by the prisoners, how they built him a playhouse. They also built the cathedral and other public buildings.

Just as one receives three distinct smells from the open sea, the lagoons, and the harbors, three different forms of life offer themselves in Noumea: the sunlit physical life, swimming, boating and other sports; the marine life, endlessly fascinating; and the Oceanic art visible in the museum. Here one becomes aware that New Caledonia is a mysterious land, much of it unexplored. Its carved petroglyphs have not yet been deciphered.

It is through the indigenous art that one becomes aware of a people who have not lost their sense of beauty as Western culture has. Our protective lightning rods are always plain and resemble antennae. For the Melanesians, the carved slender wooden tips at the top of their huts become extraordinary symbols of protective figures, stylized old men of wisdom, suggestive of compassion and benediction. Masks of wood and feathers represent the spiritual chief; tools, axes, money, clubs, spears, pirogues, dishes, spoons, knives, are all objects to be decorated, painted, sculptured, sometimes inlaid with mother-of-pearl. There is a case filled with magic stones selected for their suggestive shapes: phallic stones for aphrodisiacs, womblike stones for fertility, stones capable of bringing sun or rain or helping navigation, others demonic, dangerous, bringing cyclones, illness, death. Some large stones are tied to the end of a club to make a casse-tête. The Melanesians have a genius for dressing themselves in natural products such as skirts of jute or tapa cloth made from banyan tree roots or the bark of the mulberry tree. The tips of war spears are carved of human bones. Wooden dishes are carved in the shape of fish or turtles— all these made without the help of the tools we know. Jade is sharpened to serve as a hatchet.

The native art makes one wish for a three-day tour of the

island with taxi driver J. Bizien, who has driven a truck for twenty years, supplying the outer villages with foodstuffs, and who knows all the tribes and the tribal chiefs.

The fruit and flower arrangements in the hotel remind one of the Japanese. In every room there is an embroidered tapestry by Aloi Pilioko, the Polynesian artist now celebrated for his painting, sketches, needlework, in the primitive style of an Oceanic Picasso. There are also murals by Michoutouchkine, the well-known painter and collector of Oceanic art.

Two women stand out as symbols of the many aspects of New Caledonia. One is Dr. Catala-Stucki (her husband insists that she use her maiden name with his), the handsome, sturdy, dynamic wife of Dr. Catala and his collaborator in the creation of the aquarium. She is an oceanographer, a scientist, and a deep-sea diver. She took part in the most dangerous diving expeditions for corals and fish. Now in her sixties, she still dives every day for the particular marine food necessary for the aquarium fish. She radiates a passion for her work, for their mutual achievement, accomplished out of personal devotion and energy. Much has been written about this remarkable couple, but the most accurate and memorable descriptions of Dr. Catala-Stucki's work are found in her husband's own book, *Carnaval sous la mer*, for he has a gift for description and a sense of humor about marine life which is that of an artist and poet as well as scientist.

The other woman is Janine Tabuteau, the wife of the director of tourism in Noumea. She symbolizes the mixture of races, which prefigures the future of a world now able to uproot itself, roam, and bring the essence and quality of many cultures into one person. Janine is French, Indonesian, Chinese, and Russian. She did not at first appreciate the exotic beauty this created, the conflicts which gave depth to her character. At seventeen, when she went to Paris, she asked to have her luxuriant, long, black hair cut "like everyone else's," but the hairdresser refused. Everyone urged her to accept her distinctive appearance, her mixture of reticence and modern dynamism. She has learned to be a cook of exquisite Chinese dishes, to accept her unique beauty, to manage a company of building materials, to consider architecture and decoration as extensions of this company. It is strange to see her behind an executive desk, with her soft Indonesian voice, her French organizational power. In the evening, she goes home, dons an Indonesian skirt, and cooks an amazing dinner for friends. I feel somehow that she indicates the future, the possibility of remaining an exotic woman, not like everyone else, and yet taking an active part in the modern business world.

Over the coral reefs, half an hour from Noumea, lies the Isle of Pines, a volcanic island eroded by the sea. The sea between the two islands is dotted with atolls, isolated ring- or crescent-shaped reefs enclosing lagoons. The hotel, Relais de Kanumera, with its appealing native architecture, is built right on a lagoon. Separate bungalows are scattered among the overwhelming umbrella-shaped buni trees. From the hotel one sees a tiny volcanic island, overgrown with lush vegetation, shaped like a basket, while the sea undermines its base. The native children dive from it. At night it looks like a ship; at other times the vegetation makes it look like a hairbrush.

The remarkable hotel chef cooks in an open house, and his barbeque is a giant pit outside. It is strange, so far from Paris, to find the classic French cuisine, but the chef adds tropical creations of his own, like baked papaya filled with custard.

The Isle of Pines has flora not seen anywhere else in the world. It, too, was invaded by the sandalwood traders, the whalers, the missionaries. The French Catholic missionaries stayed on, and now on Sunday the entire population of the tiny island appears at the church. Here, watching the women, I can see how varied the short mumus are, all flowers, leaves, fruit, in primary colors. Some wear bands over their hair similar to the American Indians. Next to the church, standing alone, is a gigantic Cook pine, unbelievably tall and straight, as impressive as a cathedral.

When it was discovered that the political prisoners could disappear into the vast forests of New Caledonia, they were sent to the tiny Isle of Pines instead. The prison is now hidden from the road by almost impenetrable acacia trees and is surrounded by a high wall of stones, now breaking down. The prison itself, gloomy and forbidding, is half in ruins. The roofs are gone, but not the heavy chains bolted to the walls, nor the three layers of iron bars on the windows. The men who were sent here had been the Communards, rebelling against poor wages, the hard life of the workers. In 1870 they held Paris for three days and then were either shot or imprisoned.

In the bus, touring the island with us, is an old Frenchman. His paternal grandfather was one of the Communards but had escaped to Brittany and made a new life. But another relative had not, and when we stand by the monument erected by the prisoners to their dead brothers, the old Frenchman reads the names carved on the single stone and is moved by his family name. Among the prisoners who died on the island were women, children, and those who sought to escape by building a boat, which foundered on the coral reefs. Later, walking on the beach, famous for the whitest sand in all the world, I see the edge of a sunken boat showing through the sand and think of the prisoners who tried to escape.

For a while after leaving the prison, I am under the

haunting pain of such a place, all the more oppressive when the sky, which shows through the small, barred windows, is tropical, the smell of the lagoon so near, the flour-white sands so soft to walk on, and flowers, ferns, and tropical bushes abundant and replete with sun.

We look for sandalwood trees but find none on the island. Sandalwood was highly prized by China for its religious ceremonies. To extract the oil, the early traders tore the hearts out of the trees, ravaged them, and then moved on.

Snorkeling reveals a whole other world of fantastic beauty: red, black and blue starfish; mushroom-shaped corals; brain corals covered with sprays of flowerlike purple tips; mother-of-pearl "flowers" shaped like shells but transparent and floating on a stem as if made of silk; a ruby-red fish; the Moorish idol fish with a long, curved dorsal fin larger than its body, more like a sail or a bird's wing; black fish, each with two white spots; a velvet-black fish with white stripes, named the zebra fish; one with a jet-black tail and brown front edged with brilliant orange; others with turquoise collars. The colors are phosphorescent, transparent, jewellike. The fish hide among the corals and in the many caves made by the action of the sea on volcanic rock.

Above the surface ride the beautiful, painted pirogues, carved out of trees, with outriggers and sails. The Melanesian natives have strong bodies and the same strong feet of Gauguin's Polynesians of Tahiti.

The island is dotted with caves and grottoes. They are formed inside the volcanic depths and are filled with the familiar stalactites and stalagmites. At the very end of the Kouaouate Grotto there is an opening through which the sunlight falls like the aura over the heads of saints in Biblical pictures; and with this cascade of light are banyan roots falling like ladders down twenty feet, throwing great

---

white tentacles for fifty feet along the floor of the cave, seeking water. Here on a ledge, exposed to the dim light from above, the natives once placed the skulls of their dead. It was their belief that only the skull should be preserved. Formerly, all the caves were burial grounds.

It is difficult to forget the prisoners who built the roads we travel. But those who were pardoned and returned to France, did they remember the lagoons, the dazzling white sand, the tangled acacias, the miles of ferns, the floating islands on the Bay of Gold, the smell of sandalwood, the tranquil pirogues carrying coconuts? And the grottoes like the caves of our dreams?

My Turkish Grandmother

I was travelling on Air France to New York via Paris when
the plane ran into a flock of sea gulls and we had to stop
at Athens. At first we sat around and waited for information, looking out now and then at the airplane. Vague news
filtered out. Some passengers became anxious, fearing they
would miss their connections. Air France treated us to
dinner and wine. But after that there was a shortage of
seats, so I sat on the floor like a gypsy, together with a
charming hippie couple with whom I had made friends during the trip. He was a musician and she was a painter. They
were hitchhiking through Europe with backpacks. She was
slender and frail-looking, and I was not surprised when he
complained that her knapsack was full of vitamins. As we
sat talking about books, films, music, a very old lady ap-
proached us. She looked like my Spanish grandmother.
Dressed completely in black, old but not bent, with a face
that seemed carved of wood through which the wrinkles
appeared more like veins of the wood. She handed me a
letter she carried around her neck in a Turkish cloth bag. It
was written in exquisite French. It was a request from her
daughter to help her Turkish mother in every way possible.

From the diary of Anaïs Nin.

The daughter was receiving her doctorate in medicine at the Sorbonne and could not come to fetch her mother for the ceremony, so she had entrusted her to the care of Air France. I read the letter and translated it for my hippie friends. Although we could not talk to the old woman, it was evident that a strong, warm sympathy existed among the four of us. She wanted to sit with us. We made room for her, and she gave me her old wrinkled hand to hold. She was anxious. She did not know what had happened. She realized she would be late for her rendezvous in Paris. We looked for a Turkish passenger who would translate and explain the delay. There was none, but we found an Air France hostess who spoke a little Turkish. We thought the old lady would choose to stay with the hostess, but once the message was conveyed to her, she returned to sit with us. She adopted us. Hours passed. We were told that the plane could not be repaired, that the airline offered us a few hours of sleep in a hotel not too far away, and to be ready for an early flight on another plane. So the four of us were placed in a taxi, which caused my Turkish grandmother such anxiety that she would not let go of my hand; but her anxiety would always recede when she looked at the delicate features and soft eyes of the young woman painter, at the smile and gentleness of the musician's face, at my reassuring words in French, which she did not understand. At the hotel, she would not go into her bedroom alone, so I left our connecting doors open and explained I was right there next to her. She studied this for a while and then finally consented to lie in her bed. A few hours later, we were called and taken to our plane. Because I was changing planes in Paris, I could not take her to the home of her daughter. I had to find someone who would. Questioning the passengers, I found a woman who promised to take her in a taxi to the address in the letter. She held on to my hand until the last minute. Then she kissed me ceremoniously, kissed my hippie friends, and went on her way. Having been in her fishermen's village, I could imagine the little stone house she came from, her fisherman husband, her daughter sent to Paris to study medicine and now achieving the high status of doctor. Did she arrive in time for a ceremony which had to be translated to her? I know she arrived safely. Guarded by universal grandchildren, Turkish grandmothers always travel safely.